# THE WILD,
# UNWILLING
# WIFE

Dutton Books by Barbara Cartland
*Love Locked In*
*The Wild, Unwilling Wife*

*Barbara Cartland*

# THE WILD, UNWILLING WIFE

### E. P. DUTTON
New York

Library of Congress Cataloging in Publication Data

Cartland, Barbara, 1902-
The wild, unwilling wife.

I. Title.
PZ3.C247Wj3   [PR6005.A765]   823'.9'12   76-57981
           ISBN: 0-525-23417-9

Published simultaneously in Canada by
Clarke, Irwin & Company Limited,
Toronto and Vancouver

10 9 8 7 6 5 4 3 2 1

First Edition

## AUTHOR'S NOTE

The London Zoo originated by Sir Stafford Raffles opened in April 1826. It was to become an example to the whole world.

Before this the Tower Menagerie had been open for centuries. The entrance fee was at first a penny or, if preferred, one could bring in a live dog or cat to give as food for the animals. Lions were always the chief attraction and in the days of Elizabeth I were all named after Kings and Queens.

Towards the end of the 17th century the first hyena was shown in England and in 1739 a rhinoceros from Bengal. It was William IV who closed the Tower Menagerie after six hundred years of unbroken history. The animals went either to the Zoo or to Windsor.

Private menageries then became unfashionable only to be reinstated when owners of ancestral houses wished to attract the public. To-day the wild animals belonging to the Duke of Bedford at Woburn Abbey and those, especially the lions, owned by the Marquis of Bath at Longleat are a huge tourist attraction.

# Chapter One
## 1825

The Right Reverend Lord Bishop of Axminster sat on a hard, high-backed oak chair looking out through the diamond-paned window onto the Park.

The garden immediately around the house was a wilderness but at the same time an attractive one.

The spring daffodils were golden in the grass and made a carpet of splendour beneath the lofty oak trees.

The sun was glinting on the silver lake where the river had been widened by the Cistercian Monks when they had first built their Abbey above the river.

The Bishop, a fine-looking man with clear-cut features, was thinking back to the mediaeval times when Vernham Abbey, where he was now, had been a power for good over the whole countryside.

When Henry VIII had brought about the dissolution of the Monasteries, Sir Richard Verne had been granted the property which had added considerably to his already extensive possessions.

The Bishop, the Honourable Lorimer Verne, could trace his ancestry back to the days when the Vernes not only held positions of trust and importance at Court, but were also revered for the just and generous manner in which they ruled over their Estates.

The Bishop sighed, and as he did so there was a noise of voices in the Hall and he turned his face sharply towards the door of the room in which he sat.

He only had to wait a few seconds before the voices came nearer, the door was flung open, and the man he was waiting for came in.

"Alvaric!"

The Bishop's voice was deep as he rose to his feet.

"Hello, Uncle Lorimer," the newcomer exclaimed. "I thought you would be here. It is very good of you."

"I am delighted to welcome you home, Alvaric, and I have been waiting a long time for your return."

The younger man laughed. It seemed somehow to relieve the gloom of the dark panelled room with its low ceiling and casements which let in very little light.

"Your letter took over six months to reach me," he said. "In fact it was eventually carried over two hundred miles by native bearers before I received it."

"I thought it would be something like that which had delayed you," the Bishop said. "Come and sit down, my boy, I want to look at you."

His nephew did as he was told and seated himself on another oak chair carved with a monogram and coronet.

In the sunlight percolating through the windows, which were badly in need of a clean, the Bishop looked at his nephew with a critical eye and was delighted with what he saw.

At thirty-two Alvaric was not only exceedingly handsome, which he had always been, but he gave the impression of great strength and vital good health.

It seemed to glow from his lean body, which had not a superfluous ounce of fat on it, in the brightness of his eyes and the suntan on his skin.

The young man seemed to be waiting for his Uncle to speak and at length the Bishop said, almost as if he apologised:

"When you inherited there was nothing I could do but ask you to return as speedily as possible."

"I did my best."

"I realise that, but it seemed a long time, and now you are here I only wish I had better news for you."

Alvaric, now the eleventh Baron, raised his dark eyebrows. Then almost as if it was a question of politeness rather than curiosity he asked:

"How did my cousin die?"

"He was killed at the same time as your uncle, in fact they died together in a carriage accident."

Lord Vernham did not speak, he merely waited for the Bishop to continue.

"You might as well know the truth. Your cousin Gervaise was drunk, as he invariably was, and for some reason which is hard to ascertain he and your uncle decided to leave London late in the evening to drive here."

The Bishop paused for a moment before he said:

"My brother had taken no interest in the house or grounds for a long time, and I can only imagine that he wished to return so suddenly in order to find if there was anything else left to sell which he had previously overlooked."

"Sell?"

"As I have already said, Alvaric, I wish I had better news for you, but I would rather tell you the truth myself than that you should hear it from the Solicitors."

"I had an idea when I left England, which after all was nine years ago, that my uncle was gambling away everything that was not entailed."

"That is true," the Bishop agreed, "and Gervaise did nothing to stop him. In fact he himself spent no less than his father managed to do."

"Gambling?"

"Combined with wine and women, all of which proved to be exceedingly expensive."

"What you are telling me is that I have inherited nothing but the Estates, which they could not touch, the Abbey, which I can see is crumbling as it stands, and doubtless a number of debts."

"A mountain of them," the Bishop said.

Lord Vernham rose to his feet and walking to one of the casements opened it, noticing as he did so that the catch was broken.

He flung it wide and looked out onto what in his grandfather's day had been an attractive garden. He could see beyond it the lake where he had caught his first trout and in the background the green Park-land where he had first learnt to ride.

Vernham Abbey was full of memories for him and he thought how often when he had been living abroad, suffering from the sweltering heat or being kept awake by the noises of wild animals, he had imagined himself back in the beauty and tranquillity of the Abbey.

He had never for one moment thought that he might inherit it.

His uncle, the tenth Lord Vernham, had a son and heir who was always on the verge of getting married.

After Alvaric's father had been killed at Waterloo, his mother already having died three years previously, there had been little money and nothing to keep him in England and he decided to go abroad.

There was no-one to regret his departure, except perhaps his Uncle Lorimer, for whom he had a deep affection. He had set off on what he thought of as an adventure with all the enthusiasm of youth and without any inhibitions or ties which might limit the extent of his travels.

It had come like a bomb-shell when his uncle's letter, creased and dirty from many months' travelling, had reached him in the heart of Africa.

When he first read it he could hardly credit that it told him that he had in fact become, through two unexpected deaths, the head of the family.

His grandfather had had three sons: the oldest, Alvaric's Uncle John, was educated and trained for the position he would hold when his father died.

The second son, Alvaric's father, went into the Army, and the third, Lorimen Verne, went into the Church.

It was all part of the tradition followed by the Vernes for centuries and, as might be expected, the bulk of the family fortune was in the keeping of the holder of the title.

"What has happened to the land we owned in London?" Lord Vernham asked. "If I remember, there is Vernham Square in Bloomsbury and several streets which belong to us."

"Your uncle managed to break the agreement of Gervaise and they were sold."

"Was that legal?"

"No, but no-one felt inclined to interfere, and I imagine if they had not got the money at that particular moment one or the other of them would have gone to prison."

"Suppose you tell me what is left?"

Lord Vernham walked from the window to seat himself once again in the chair opposite his uncle.

"I am afraid what I have to tell you will come as rather a shock," the Bishop said hesitatingly. "I do not know whether you remember a man called Theobold Muir, whose lands are adjacent to the Abbey on the South side?"

"Muir?" Lord Vernham repeated reflectively. "I do seem to remember the name. Was he a friend of the family?"

"Your grandfather refused to acknowledge him when he first bought Kingsclere, the Estate of a family who had lived there for centuries."

"I presume Grandfather considered him an upstart," Lord Vernham said with a smile.

"You are quite right," the Bishop answered. "My

father could be very stiff-necked about newcomers
and apparently he disliked Theobold Muir on sight."

"What happened?" Lord Vernham enquired.

"He became a friend of your uncle's almost as soon
as he inherited. He is excessively rich and I imagine
my brother started borrowing from him as soon as they
became acquainted."

The Bishop paused as if he found it hard to speak
in such a manner of his own kith and kin.

After a moment's pause he went on:

"Whether at first Muir had any ulterior motive in
being so generous I do not know. But there is no doubt
that as the years passed he had a reason for lending
my brother any amount of money he needed for
gaming, and for buying from him everything that he
wished to sell."

Lord Vernham looked startled.

"The pictures!" he exclaimed.

"They all belong now to Theobold Muir."

Lord Vernham rose to his feet once again.

"Damit, Uncle Lorimer! Forgive my language, but
this is too much! They are family pictures. They do not
belong to one of us but to all, and anyway the majority
of them are portraits."

"Perhaps we should be grateful to Muir for keeping
the collection intact," the Bishop hazarded, but he did
not sound as if he meant it.

"What else of ours does he possess?"

"The silver."

Lord Vernham's lips tightened.

The silver was no less a part of the Verne history.
Some of it had actually belonged to the Cistercian
Monks. Other pieces had been presented by Henry
VIII and other Kings and Queens who had been served
by the family in one capacity or another.

There was silver which General Sir Roderick Verne
had taken with him in the campaigns he had fought
under Marlborough, and there was silver which had

been a personal wedding-gift from George II to Alvaric's great-great-grandfather.

He could remember it gracing the table at Christmas
and at other times when the family were all assembled
round the refectory table in the Dining-Hall where
once the Monks had eaten their frugal meals.

The huge candelabra bearing the Verne crest and
coat-of-arms had glittered and shone on cups and
bowls, dishes and vases. As a small boy he had been
fascinated by them, feeling that they were as bright as
the sunlight on the lake outside.

Lord Vernham walked across the room as if to
relieve his feelings. Then he said:

"I need not bother to ask you what has happened
to the tapestries. They were unique and so much a part
of the Abbey that I can hardly believe they are not
still hanging on the walls."

"I believe they are well cared for," the Bishop
replied.

"But they belong to this man Muir. Would it be
possible to challenge his ownership?"

The Bishop said slowly:

"No Court would restore them to you, unless you
could repay the debt which was incurred and for
which such treasures stood surety."

"How much was owed?" Alvaric asked.

The Bishop hesitated a moment before he replied:

"Something over fifty thousand pounds!"

"I do not believe it!" Lord Vernham exclaimed.

Then he looked at his uncle's face and knew there
was no doubt that the Bishop was being accurate.

He gave a deep sigh.

"So that is the end," he said, "the end of the Abbey,
the end of the Estate, and to all intents and purposes
the end of the family!"

He walked to the window again as if in need of
air, before he said:

"You have some idea of how little I possess. I have

enough to keep me in reasonable comfort and to pay
for my travels, but not enough to run this place for a
year, let alone any longer."

He paused, then said:

"Surely there must be some money coming in from
the farms."

"They are mostly empty," the Bishop replied. "Your
uncle would never do any repairs, and when the tenants
died or left there was no Agent to find new ones. Many
of the farm-houses are roofless and it would need ex-
ceptionally fine farmers to get the land back into good
heart."

"And yet I remember people saying there were no
better farms in the whole country."

"In your grandfather's day—yes."

Lord Vernham turned from the window.

"Tell me, Uncle Lorimer," he said. "What am I to
do?"

"Come and sit down, Alvaric," the Bishop said.
"There is something you can do, but it is not easy for
me to tell you what it is."

"Why?" Lord Vernham enquired.

"I think I said just now that Muir had an object in
view when he continued to lend your uncle money for
his unrestrained gambling and also to all intents and
purposes keep Gervaise in luxury."

"It sounds as if he is either a crazy philanthropist or
a fool!" Lord Vernham exclaimed.

"That is what it would appear, except for one thing,"
the Bishop replied.

"And what is that?"

"Theobold Muir has a daughter."

The Bishop spoke quietly but Lord Vernham started
as if at a pistol-shot.

"A daughter?" he queried.

"She was engaged to Gervaise before he died."

"I see!" Lord Vernham said slowly. "So that is what
Muir wanted, his daughter as mistress of Vernham

Abbey. He certainly was prepared to pay heavily for the privilege."

"It is in fact an obsession with him," the Bishop said, "as strong and unrestrained as the obsession your uncle had for gaming. It is the ambition of his life and he will never rest until he has attained it."

Lord Vernham was very still. Then his dark eyes met those of his uncle and there was a question in them which he had no need to put into words.

"I saw Muir yesterday," the Bishop said quietly. "He informed me that if you are prepared to marry his daughter, his wedding-present to you will be the return of everything he now holds which once belonged to the Abbey. He is also willing to restore the house, grounds, and the farms."

Lord Vernham drew in his breath audibly.

"I understand," the Bishop went on, "that his daughter, Jarita, already owns a fortune of some three hundred thousand pounds, and when her father dies she will inherit his entire wealth."

"Are you putting this proposition before me quite seriously?" Lord Vernham asked.

"I am telling you what Muir is prepared to do and I believe him to be a man of his word."

"But this girl—can she really transfer her affections so quickly from one man to another?"

"I doubt if she has much say in what she does or does not do," the Bishop replied drily, "and anyone who was prepared to marry Gervaise will doubtless find you a very welcome exchange."

Lord Vernham was once again walking across the room.

There were only a few thread-bare rugs on the wooden floor and his footsteps seemed to make an ominous sound almost like the tread of a funeral-bearer.

"It is too much! Too much to ask of any man!" he cried. "I have been free, Uncle Lorimer. I have been my own master. If I am honest, much as I revere the family and know full well what it means in the lives of all of us, I have no wish to be sacrificed on the altar of tradition."

"I can understand that," the Bishop said sympathetically, "but there is such a thing, Alvaric, as duty. Whatever you may feel or think, you are now Lord Vernham, and as such the head of the family."

"What is left of it."

"There are in fact well over fifty Vernes who can claim a close relationship with us," the Bishop explained, "and a large number, indeed hundreds of others, in the ever-widening circle produced by marriages and births."

"And you think this place means anything to them?"

"It means what it means to you and me," the Bishop said. "It is the centre to which they belong and to which, whatever happens in their personal lives, they feel an allegiance and a loyalty. There have been weak, wicked Vernes, and those like your uncle who dissipated their inheritance and were not worthy of the family name. But there are many, as you know, whose acts of gallantry have been told and retold until they shine like a brilliant light to inspire the children who come after us."

The Bishop spoke with a sincerity in his voice that was very moving, and after a moment his nephew said quietly:

"I know now what you are urging me to do."

"Henry of Navarre said that Paris was well worth a Mass," the Bishop replied. "I think that when you consider it, Alvaric, you will come to the conclusion that the Abbey is worth a marriage."

"The whole idea fills me with horror!" Lord Vernham exclaimed. "It is not just that it would be an arranged marriage. This is something that has happened, as I well know, for centuries amongst the noble

families, and in the East no girl sees her bridegroom
until after they are wed."

He drew in his breath before he added:

"But this girl, this daughter of Theobold Muir, was
engaged to my cousin."

"Gervaise would doubtless have married the daughter
of the devil himself if she was well endowed," the
Bishop said sarcastically.

As if he could not help himself Lord Vernham
laughed.

"That is the sort of remark, Uncle Lorimer, that has
always made me love you. Any other man in your
position might have had the same thought but would
have dolled it up in Episcopal language!"

The Bishop's eyes twinkled.

"I am speaking to you at the moment, Alvaric, not
as a Bishop but as a Verne. I make no bones about
saying that Gervaise disgusted me, and if it were not
a very un-Christian thing to say I would tell you that
the world is a cleaner and better place because he has
left it."

"As bad as that?" Lord Vernham asked, raising his
eye-brows.

"Worse!" the Bishop said briefly. "There will be
plenty of people to tell you of your cousin's behaviour
and there is no need for me to elaborate on it. Let me
say that I am only astonished—or rather appalled—
that any father could have wished his daughter to marry
Gervaise."

"Which brings us back to Theobold Muir," Lord
Vernham said.

"Exactly!"

"I suppose you expect me to go and see him?"

"The only alternative is for you to wash your hands
of the whole unsavoury mess and return to where you
came from. Doubtless in the wilds of Africa you will
be able to forget the Abbey and it will fall gradually
to the ground."

The Bishop did not speak dramatically, which made his quiet voice somehow more convincing.

Once again Lord Vernham rose to go to the window and look out.

He thought that the daffodils were even more golden than he remembered, and he was certain that down by the edge of the lake the kingcups would be golden too.

He used to pick them for his grandmother and had been bitterly disappointed when they withered and died almost before he could carry them back to the house.

He wondered if the trout were lying in the shadows of the willow trees.

Once when he was a little boy one of the gardeners had shown him how to tickle them, and he had used the skill he had learned then on various occasions when he had been camping in some far-off part of the world and had wanted a fish to eat.

But nothing had ever tasted quite so delicious as the trout from the lake at Vernham, just as no fruit, however exotic, had ever equalled the peaches he had stolen, when the gardener was not looking, from the great walled-in kitchen-garden which lay beyond the stables.

He supposed now the kitchen-garden would be full of weeds and the stables empty of horses, and there would be no groom making a whistling sound between his teeth as he rubbed down a shining black, brown, or chestnut coat.

Yes, the stables would be very quiet with only the ghosts of horses' heads to look over the half-doors, reaching out greedily for a carrot or a piece of apple.

And there would be ghosts in the long Picture Gallery too, which had been a perfect place not only for hide-and-seek, but for sliding along the polished floors.

"Get along with you, Master Alvaric," the housemaids would say. "Coming in here, and messing up the place with your dirty boots!"

But there was always a gingerbread cake waiting for

him in the kitchen, or a big muscate grape in the Pantry.

When he was older the cooks used to pack slices from the hams hanging from the rafters to take out hunting and which fitted in a little silver box into a special place in his saddle.

There would be memories, he knew, in every part of the house, in every part of the grounds.

There was the copse where he had shot his first pheasant—he could remember the thrill of it still! The place in the Park where he had ferreted with one of the game-keepers and the agony it had been when his own special ferret had got stuck down a hole and he had thought he would never see it again.

The Abbey had been the center of his childhood, and although his parents had a house on the other side of the village it was always the Abbey which had drawn him, and both his grandfather and grandmother had liked to have him there.

"You must not let Alvaric be a nuisance to you," he could hear his mother say in her sweet voice.

"Alvaric is never a nuisance," his grandmother had replied. "He is a real Verne, and his grandfather was saying only last night he is the best rider of the whole family. There is no-one to touch him!"

How proud he had been riding over the land which he had felt in a way he owned simply because he was a Verne.

He tried to be friendly with Gervaise, but his cousin already resented him.

"You always have the best horses," Gervaise had stormed on one occasion. "That is why you keep in the front of the field and are in at the kill!"

The real reason was that Gervaise was an inferior rider, but Alvaric had been far too tactful to say so.

"Follow me, Gervaise," he said, "and we will both leave the rest behind!"

But Gervaise had merely looked sulky. He did not want to share anything with his older cousin.

This was one of the reasons, Lord Vernham knew now, why he had gone abroad after his uncle's death.

He would have found it difficult not to remonstrate with Gervaise at the way he treated the servants, the tenants, the people who had lived on the Estate all their lives and to whom it meant home.

His sense of irritation at his uncle's gaming and his neglect of the Abbey had been increasing every year as he grew older.

He began to notice things which needed repairing but were left undone. The pensions for the old retainers were not as generous as they should have been. Cottages that were dilapidated were left empty instead of being repaired.

It had been brought home to him all too clearly that it was not his business to interfere and that his name gave him no authority where the Abbey was concerned.

He had gone abroad, but he had been unable to forget. The Abbey had haunted him and he knew now if he left it again, if he abandoned it to its fate, it would haunt him until he died.

And yet something within him rebelled violently and obstinately against being tied to anyone's apron strings.

He had no wish to be married. There had been many women in his life, but they had all sooner or later become dispensable and he had parted from them with little regret.

To be tied to one woman would be unbearable, and all the more so because she was the daughter of the man who to all intents and purposes had bought the Abbey.

It made him feel sick to think of anyone acquiring the treasures one by one, taking the pictures and the tapestries from the walls, the silver from the great safe which stood in the Butler's Pantry, the china, the glass,

the objets d'art with which his grandmother had surrounded herself in her bed-room and her *Boudoir*.

There was no doubt that from that point of view
Theobold Muir had a very strong basis from which to
bargain, and by comparison Alvaric's freedom seemed
a very small price to pay for it all.

"Well, there is one consolation about it all," he said
aloud, knowing that neither he nor his uncle had
spoken for a long time.

"What is that?" the Bishop enquired.

"There is plenty of room here for my animals."

"Your animals?" the Bishop sounded surprised.

"To be precise, two cheetahs, two lions, and quite a
number of parrots!"

"You brought them back with you?"

"I could not leave them behind. I have tamed them,
and to turn them back into the wild after they have
been with me for so many years would end inevitably in
their being killed by other animals."

"Do you imagine they will fit into the English land-
scape?"

"It is nothing new to have menageries in England,
Uncle Lorimer, as you well know. Julius Caesar was
surprised to find that the ancient Britons kept animals
for pleasure. Noblemen have had housed collections of
animals all down the centuries. There is a record of
one of them receiving a bear from the son of William
the Conqueror."

He smilled and went on:

"As a little boy I used to love the story of the famous
white bear at the Tower of London which was trans-
ferred there from Henry III's collection at Woodstock."

"I forget the tale," the Bishop murmured.

"The City's Sheriffs were obliged to provide it with
a muzzle, an iron chain, and a stout rope, and to save
expense it was taken daily down to the Thames to fish
for its own supper."

The Bishop laughed.

"Now I recall that at Woodstock in the year 1100 there were lions, leopards, camels, and lynxes."

"England was only copying the example of Italy," Lord Vernham replied. "If you remember, Uncle Lorimer, the menagerie at Florence was the pride of the City and Pope Leo X actually housed his wild animals in the Vatican."

"I remember reading about it," the Bishop said, "and that Leonardo da Vinci kept the animals he drew so brilliantly!"

"I wish I could have brought more home with me," Lord Vernham remarked. "I considered including an ostrich but the poor things do not travel well."

"And your lions and cheetahs are none the worse for the journey?"

"They seemed well, if a little nervous, when I left them. They are being conveyed here on wagons, and that, as you can imagine, will take several days more. I came by post-chaise as I knew you were waiting for me."

"I received your message saying that you had arrived in Southampton," the Bishop said, "and could not imagine why you had not come at once in person."

"I had to see to the unloading of my own special family," Lord Vernham replied. "I shall look forward, Uncle Lorimer, to introducing them to you. I am sure that the parrots, at any rate, will find you, like St. Francis, irresistible!"

The Bishop laughed.

"As a boy you were always full of surprises, Alvaric, and you surprise me now. I somehow did not think of you keeping wild animals as pets. I always thought of you shooting game, as you used to do in your father's day."

"Perhaps it was living with Buddhists that made me feel I no longer had any wish to take life," Lord Vernham replied. "At times it is inevitable because my family has to eat and I shall not be able to allow them

to do their own hunting in England. But killing for food
is a very different thing from killing for pleasure."

"Once again I can only say you surprise me, Alvaric!"

"Not half as much as you have surprised me," Lord
Vernham replied. "And now, Uncle Lorimer, do you
think there is any chance of our having a drink together? I admit after my journey to feeling very
thirsty."

"My dear boy, how remiss of me!" the Bishop exclaimed. "I should have thought of it sooner, but I was
in fact so perturbed by what I had to tell you that it
put every other thought out of my mind."

He rose to his feet.

"I did in fact bring some wine with me and we will
find it in the Dining-Room, where my servants have
laid out a cold collation, for I thought you might be
hungry."

"As indeed I am!" Lord Vernham replied. "I am
extremely grateful to you, Uncle Lorimer."

They walked from the room in which they had been
sitting down a corridor empty of all furniture and pictures to the great Dining-Hall.

Lord Vernham remembered the long refectory table
which would never have fitted into anyone else's house,
and at which fifty Monks had eaten with their Prior at
the head.

The Minstrels' Gallery had been added at a much
later date, the screen that hid the players being finely
carved.

The huge open fireplace had been ornamented with
a magnificent marble mantelshelf and was the work of
a seventeenth-century craftsman.

The coat-of-arms of the Vernes and those of some
of the families with which they had been united in
marriage were set in coloured glass in several of the
long windows.

But both the Bishop and Lord Vernham were for

the moment more concerned with the meal which lay
at one end of the long refectory table, laid out neatly
on a white linen cloth, while in a silver ice-bucket there
reposed two bottles of wine,

"Though a bachelor, Uncle Lorimer," Lord Vernham said, "you seem to enjoy all the comforts of a
married man."

"Not all of them, dear boy, but at least some," the
Bishop agreed. "I think we will both feel a little calmer
when we have eaten and drunk. What we have experienced this morning has been, to say the least of it, dis-
turbing."

"I can only thank you for telling me yourself," Lord
Vernham said. "As you surmised, I would have hated
to learn what has happened from an outsider."

"That is what I thought," the Bishop said.

He sat down as if it was his right at the head of the
table and for a moment his hands were joined together
in prayer. Then he began to cut with a silver knife the
fine red salmon which lay on a silver dish in front of
him.

"You must forgive me, Alvaric, if I remind you that
today is Friday, and I am restricted to fish."

"As it happens I am very partial to salmon," Lord
Vernham replied.

"It is particularly good at this time of the year," the
Bishop replied, helping first his nephew and then himself.

"Shall I open the wine?" Lord Vernham asked.

"Please do," the Bishop agreed. "I thought it would
be more comfortable if we waited on ourselves. It is
impossible to converse when either my Chaplain or my
servants are listening to everything we say."

"I agree," Lord Vernham said, "and I assure you I
am very used to waiting on myself, at any rate until I
taught the natives, wherever I was camping, how to give
me some type of service."

He smiled as he added:

"It was usually pretty rough."

"You appear to have thrived on it."

"I never felt better! I have led a hard life, but a very rewarding one."

"I shall want to hear all about it, and there is a great deal for you to learn about this country."

"So I gather, but those I ask wish to tell me only of the indiscretions and the extravagances of the King."

"His Majesty has certainly been extravagant all his life," the Bishop agreed. "At the same time, having once got into debt when he was young, it was almost impossible for him ever to be free of it."

"I wish my uncle, if he were alive, could offer the same excuse," Alvaric said.

"The excesses are not in the least similar," the Bishop said sharply. "The King's main extravagance has been in building and in buying pictures and statues. He had spent a fortune, Alvaric, on Carlton House, and another on the Royal Pavilion at Brighton. But who knows, posterity may find that they are worth more than he paid for them."

"While my uncle merely wasted his money on the green-baize tables," Lord Vernham said bitterly, "with nothing to show for it but a debt that I have to pay on his behalf."

"Exactly!" the Bishop agreed. "And, Alvaric, let me drink your health and tell you that in making the decision you have I consider you are behaving not only like a gentleman but also as a Verne."

Lord Vernham knew that he could receive no higher praise and as his uncle raised his glass to him he said with a twinkle in his eye:

"Thank you, Uncle Lorimer, but I cannot help feeling you would not be so sanguine about the future if it were you who had to marry Theobold Muir's daughter, and not I!"

"That is true," the Bishop agreed, "but you never

know, Alvaric, she may turn out to be much pleasanter than you expect."

"I expect nothing," Lord Vernham replied, "but all the same, tell me what she is like."

"I am afraid I have never seen her," the Bishop answered.

"Then I am really and truly taking on a 'pig in a poke,' " Lord Vernham said. "She may be squint-eyed and pock-marked. You have not concerned yourself with that? If she is, I swear to you that I will turn her over to the Church and they shall take charge of her."

"Now, Alvaric," the Bishop said calmly, "you are imagining a lot of things which we both know have no foundation in fact. As it happens, Theobold Muir, though one may dislike him, is a very presentable-looking man."

He looked at his nephew's expression and added:

"Surprisingly, because one might have thought otherwise, he is a gentleman and comes of good stock. I have taken the trouble to find out."

"That is undoubtedly reassuring," Lord Vernham said, and although his voice was sarcastic the Bishop felt that he was slightly relieved.

"What is more," the Bishop continued, as if he was determined to find pleasing things to say, "Theobold Muir undoubtedly has good taste. I called at his house yesterday at his invitation, and although the luxury of Kingsclere is overwhelming, there is nothing which offends the eye."

"You might have asked to see his daughter," Lord Vernham said, pouring both the Bishop and himself another glass of wine.

"As a matter of fact, I thought Theobold Muir would suggest it," the Bishop said, "but when he did not offer to do so I felt slightly embarrassed to suggest it myself. It would have seemed almost as if I were spying out the land on your behalf."

"That is exactly what I should have liked you to do."

"My dear boy, there are many things I would wish to do for you, but you must do your own courting."

"Courting!" Lord Vernham exclaimed. "There is no question of that! I shall just sign on the dotted line, as it were, and the possessions I require will be handed across the table in return for my coronet—an object which I cannot help feeling will never fit very comfortably on my head."

"Nonsense!" the Bishop said sharply. "You are everything, Alvaric, that one would hope a Peer to be. The only difference from most of them being that you are so outrageously healthy!"

Lord Vernham threw back his head and laughed.

"I like your adverb, Uncle Lorimer, and I agree with you. It is outrageous for a nobleman to be as healthy as I am! I should be pale and hollow-eyed from drinking all night and half blind from ruining my eye-sight staring at the cards. I should be thin from dissipation and languid from anaemia."

He laughed again and continued:

"I shall not fit into the House of Lords with any comfort, as you are undoubtedly aware."

"I think you are exactly what the Lords has needed for some time," the Bishop contradicted. "An injection of fresh air and good common sense is in my opinion much needed amongst the younger members of the House."

"As far as I am concerned it will go on lacking it," Lord Vernham replied. "There is enough to keep me occupied here for the next five years, and I intend to make one thing very clear—while I am prepared to spend my future father-in-law's money on the Estate, I will not allow him to interfere with the running of it. That will rest on me—and me alone!"

"It may be a battle of wills, or it may not," the Bishop said reflectively, "but I have a feeling that Theobold Muir, having got his own way with regard to a title for his daughter and an Estate on which her fortune can be expended, will withdraw into the background."

"I hope you are right," Lord Vernham said. "I will brook no interference from anyone, and certainly not from my wife, however rich she may be!"

# Chapter Two

"I have had the tapestries repaired and the silver restored and cleaned," Theobold Muir said. "The Goldsmiths and Silversmith to whom I took it said they had never in their lives seen such magnificent pieces so neglected."

Lord Vernham did not reply.

Although he was quite aware that Mr. Muir was expecting to be thanked, he found it difficult to speak to him with any semblance of politeness.

He could not explain it even to himself but he had known that, like his grandfather, as soon as he met Theobold Muir he took an instantaneous dislike to him.

On the face of it, it seemed quite unreasonable.

Theobold Muir was, as the Bishop had said, a tall, rather handsome man who was undoubtedly a gentleman, but during his time abroad Lord Vernham had grown used to trusting his instinct in assessing a man's character.

When he was miles off the beaten track in a primitive part of Africa he had to know whom he could trust and whom he could not, using a sense which he had heard referred to in the East as the "Third Eye."

He often thought to himself that the civilised world

23

had grown too used to accepting references for servants, to adhering to other people's opinions in business, and even being a little uncertain what one felt personally about one's contemporaries and equals.

He therefore prided himself that after many years of employing natives and having to trust them not only with his possessions but often with his life, he seldom, if ever, made a mistake.

He had known as soon as he shook hands with Theobold Muir that he was a man he distrusted and disliked.

What was more, if he had followed his natural impulse he would immediately have left Kingsclere and endeavoured, as his grandfather had done, never again to have any communication with its owner.

But unfortunately this was not a question of personal prejudice, but something which concerned the Abbey and the Estate, and therefore ceased to be his own problem.

Mr. Muir was everything that was affable.

He led Lord Vernham into rooms which, as the Bishop had said, were furnished magnificently and in perfect taste.

Lord Vernham could not help looking with surprise at some of the pictures which he recognised as well-known masterpieces.

He was also aware that the furniture was worthy of a Royal setting and that a man who had acquired such treasures must have an exceptional knowledge of them.

In ordinary circumstances, he thought, he would have found it pleasing to have a neighbour who was interested in the things that he had been brought up to admire and appreciate and which were very much a part of his life.

It was his grandfather who had instructed him about paintings and his grandmother who had taught him the history of the tapestries which had hung on the walls of the Abbey and which had been added to all down the ages by a succession of Vernes.

Some of them even depicted scenes from the family history and had been woven especially for the owner of the Abbey of that particular period.

Several had been looted during wars on the Continent in which one Verne or another had always been engaged.

Although they made a unique and one of the most valuable collections in the whole length and breadth of England, and Lord Vernham could not help, as he moved through the spacious Salons of Kingsclere, expecting to see the Verne tapestries.

"You have been in Africa, I believe," Theobold Muir was saying as they seated themselves in Queen Anne winged arm-chairs on either side of the marble-framed fireplace.

Footmen wearing a quiet but distinctive livery offered them glasses of wine.

The wine was perfect and Lord Vernham took a sip appreciatively before he replied:

"Yes, I have been travelling over the world for some years and I was in fact deep in what might be called the heart of Africa when I learnt of my uncle's death."

"A great tragedy!" Mr. Muir remarked. "In fact doubly so, since your cousin died at the same time."

Lord Vernham inclined his head but could not bring himself to prejure the truth by agreeing that Gervaise's death was a tragedy.

"Your uncle will have told you," Theobold Muir went on, "that your cousin Gervaise was betrothed to my daughter."

"So I understand."

"It had not been announced, but we had discussed the terms of a marriage contract which I may say was very much to your cousin's satisfaction."

Lord Vernham did not speak. He found himself bristling almost, he thought, as if he were an animal, and his hackles were rising at the manner in which this stranger was talking.

"I will be frank with you, My Lord," Theobold Muir continued, "and say that to me the Abbey has always personified everything that is most admirable in British architecture, while its atmosphere has an appeal that I find quite irresistible."

He paused, and as Lord Vernham did not reply, he continued:

"That was why I was ready to help your uncle by offering him the loans he needed so badly so that he could continue with his favourite occupation of gambling."

"A very expensive one!" Lord Vernham remarked drily.

"I agree with you, but there is no need for me to tell you that nothing I could have said would have prevented him from continuing to believe that his luck must change. If I had not bought what he wished to sell, there would have been many other purchasers."

This was undoubtedly true and with an effort Lord Vernham strove to overcome his prejudice against the man who really believed that he had done the family a service.

"I had not anticipated, in fact," Theobold Muir went on, "that your uncle would have such abysmally bad luck and seldom, if ever, turn up a winning card."

He sighed.

"I realise of course that it was singularly unfortunate for your family, who loved and revered the Abbey."

"I understand from the Bishop that you have bought practically everything my uncle tried to sell."

"That is true," Theobold Muir replied, "and the few pictures he disposed of before we came to an arrangement I managed to buy back, although I was forced to pay a very much higher sum for them than your uncle had received."

There was silence and again Lord Vernham tried to

force some expression of gratitude to his lips but found
it impossible.

"You will therefore find that all the treasures of the
Abbey are now safely stored in this house," Theobold
Muir said, and there was a note of triumph in his voice.
"They have been attended to by experts, they have
been repaired and a number of them were, I may say,
urgently in need of it. When they are restored to where
they belong it will undoubtedly give the house a new
beauty."

"I am sure I speak for the whole family when I say
that we are very much in your debt," Lord Vernham
managed to say.

A smile curved Theobold Muir's lips and as it did
so Lord Vernham realised why he disliked and mis-
trusted the man.

He had always thought that mouths were very reveal-
ing and there was no doubt that despite his handsome
features Mr. Muir's mouth dominated his face and his
expression.

There was something cruel in the thin lips and when
they shut in a hard line Lord Vernham knew that he
was a man of boundless determination; a man who
would let nothing and nobody stand in his way.

'There is something sinister about him,' he thought
to himself, then felt he was being absurd.

"Would you wish to see where I have housed these
treasures?" Theobold Muir was asking.

Lord Vernham shook his head.

"I think I would prefer to wait until they are returned
to their rightful home," he said slowly.

There was a light in the eyes of the man opposite
him which was unmistakable.

"Your uncle has told you of my terms?"

"That I should marry your daughter?"

"Exactly!"

"I think, Mr. Muir, you leave me little chance of
refusing," Lord Vernham said. "I understand there is

also a debt of some fifty thousand pounds owed to you
by my late uncle and cousin."

"That is true," Mr. Muir agreed, "but that will be
part of the marriage contract. Besides which, I have
also agreed to restore the Abbey, the farms, and land
into working order."

"I can only say that you are very generous."

Theobold Muir rose from the chair to stand with his
back to the mantelshelf.

"Your uncle did not ask me, but I imagine you are
curious, My Lord, as to how I have acquired my
wealth."

"I think neither of us would wish to appear in-
quisitive," Lord Vernham murmured.

"I am not ashamed to say that I worked for a great
deal of it," Theobold Muir said. "My father, who was a
small country Squire in Yorkshire, left me a few thousand pounds and a large acreage of land which was
unproductive. I was quite young at the time, but I
realised it was not enough for what I wanted."

He glanced round the room with an expression that
was almost one of triumph before he continued:

"I bought property, My Lord—property in Liver-
pool, Manchester, and Leeds—and because I was certain that sooner or later these towns would expand, I
also purchased cotton mills and invested in shipping."

He paused before he added:

"That was very profitable for some years."

He did not say any more on that subect, and yet in
that moment Lord Vernham knew irrefutably that the
shipping in which he had been engaged had been the
slave trade.

This had been immensely profitable at the end of the
last century, and it was only after an outcry had risen
all over the world at the cruelty involved in such ne-
farious trading that public opinion began to veer against
it.

'This man is cruel to the point of brutality,' Lord Vernham thought.

But he knew that he dared not express his opinion, so he merely listened as Theobold Muir continued:

"Unlike your uncle, I was very fortunate. Everything I touched seemed to turn to gold, and at a rough estimate I am today worth, I suppose, about four million pounds!"

It was hard for Lord Vernham not to gasp.

This was a bigger fortune than he had ever dreamt the man might have, and he could understand that in proportion the debt owed by his uncle was not a matter for great concern.

"You will appreciate, therefore," Theobold Muir said, "that I want the best for my only child—my daughter, Jarita."

"And you thought my cousin Gervaise could provide that?"

It was something he should not have said, but the words came involuntarily and irrepressibly to his lips.

"Your cousin would one day have been Lord Vernham and the owner of the Abbey. That is what concerned me," Mr. Muir replied. "I think, moreover, although I may have been optimistic, that once he was married to Jarita I could have made certain that he behaved himself, in certain directions at any rate."

Lord Vernham squared his chin.

"What you would have done about my cousin," he said, "is not my concern. I think I should make it clear, Mr. Muir, that I would brook no interference in my private life, however beholden I might be to you as regards my house and my property."

There was a look of amusement on the older man's face as he replied:

"I am not a fool, My Lord. I am well aware that you are a very different proposition from your cousin. To set your mind at rest, may I say that having seen you and listened to what your uncle had to say about you I am quite sure that once the Abbey and the Estate are put in order you will need no further help."

"Thank you."

There was a little pause. Then Mr. Muir walked to a side-table on which there reposed a number of rolled-up parchments.

"I was going to suggest," he said, "that we should peruse these together, but I think now that you would rather read them when you are alone. Any objections, amendments, or alterations you require can be dealt with by my Attorneys, whom I will ask to call on you tomorrow."

"Thank you," Lord Vernham said again. "And now, before we go any further, I would like to meet your daughter."

He thought, although he was not sure, that Mr. Muir look surprised, but without making any comment he picked up a small gold bell which stood on a side-table and rang it.

Instantly the door of the Salon opened.

"Ask Miss Jarita to come here immediately!" he ordered.

"Very good, Sir."

As the door closed Mr. Muir said:

"Jarita is very young and, may I say, has no idea of the negotiations that have taken place between your uncle and myself."

"She made no objection to marrying my cousin?" Lord Vernham questioned.

"Jarita does as I tell her," Mr. Muir replied. "She met him once and I informed her that they would be officially engaged as soon as certain formalities had taken place. When she learnt of his death, she not unnaturally did not grieve for him very deeply."

"She met him only once?" Lord Vernham queried. "I hope I shall have the opportunity of getting to know Miss Muir before our marriage takes place."

"I consider that quite unnecessary!"

The words were sharp and Lord Vernham looked at his host in astonishment.

"I may seem unconventional," Mr. Muir said, "but I consider long engagements and what is called 'courtship' between two young people to be in most cases unsettling and undesirable. Besides, I would like to point out to you, My Lord, that the sooner you are married the sooner the restoration of the Abbey can begin."

The words were spoken with all geniality, but Lord Vernham was aware that there was a threat behind them.

Nothing, he was to understand, would be done, not one finger would be raised to restore the Abbey, farms, or land, until Jarita Muir became Lady Vernham.

There was a hint of the iron that lay beneath the smiling surface; there was a sense of purpose and determination that was inescapable.

In that moment Lord Vernham longed more than he had ever longed for anything before to rise to his feet and tell Mr. Muir to go to hell.

Not to be trusted by such a man was, he thought, a greater insult than he had ever before encountered in his whole life.

Yet there was nothing he could do about it, and because he had exercised self-control all his life he managed to ask in a calm, expressionless voice:

"Are you suggesting, Mr. Muir, that we should be married immediately?"

"Why not?"

"It seems somewhat precipitate."

"You forget you have been a long time returning to England and the Abbey and its Estates have deteriorated still further with no-one in authority."

"I can understand that."

"I suggest that you marry within the next few days," Mr. Muir went on. "You could then go on your honeymoon and I will put an army of workmen in to get the house into some semblance of order before you return."

"I would not agree to that," Lord Vernham replied. "If you insist on an immediate marriage, I could not contemplate going away so soon after returning to England."

He saw that Theobold Muir was surprised at his answer, and at the same time was considering it.

"One of the reasons why I cannot leave concerns my animals."

The older man raised his eye-brows.

"Like my uncle, you may be surprised," Lord Vernham said, "but I have brought back with me what is to be the foundation of a menagerie, and I could trust no-one but myself to see to their well-being in what to them is a strange country and an unaccustomed climate."

"You intend to have a menagerie at the Abbey?"

"I do!" Lord Vernham said firmly. "It is, I may say, an ambition I have had since I was a boy, and I was fascinated before I left the country by the menagerie in the Park near Sandpit Gate, where the Duke of Cumberland kept a variety of wild beasts."

"I remember hearing of the animal combats that take place there," Mr. Muir murmured reflectively. "I believe on one occasion His Grace pitted a tiger against a stag."

"A disgusting and barbarous performance!" Lord Vernham said. "The animals were, however, better housed than they were in Polito's Royal Menagerie at the Exeter Change in the Strand."

"I went there quite recently with one of my friends from the north, to see the white tiger," Mr. Muir said. "I cannot say that I am particularly enamoured of wild animals, but he was extremely enthusiastic about them."

"As I am."

"Well, every man to his hobby," Mr. Muir remarked,

"and of course I understand and respect your wish to remain at the Abbey while the renovations are in progress, although I cannot believe it will be very comfortable."

"I have endured many discomforts in the last few years," Lord Vernham remarked with a smile.

Mr. Muir was about to make a further comment when the door opened and without any announcement a girl came into the room.

As it happened, while they had been talking Lord Vernham had risen to set down his empty glass on the silver tray which held the decanter.

He was therefore not looking towards the door as the girl came in, and only as Theobold Muir exclaimed: "Jarita!" did he turn to look at his future wife.

He saw that she was very slender and that her fair hair held touches of red.

He realised too that she was expensively and fashionably dressed, but she bent her head so low that he could not see her face.

"This is Jarita, My Lord," Mr. Muir explained unnecessarily. Then he said to his daughter:

"This, Jarita, is your future husband!"

Lord Vernham bowed, and Jarita, standing only a little way inside the Salon, made a deep curtsey.

He waited as she did so for her to look up at him, but as she rose her head was still lowered and he had the impression only of very white skin and an oval forehead.

"That will be all, Jarita!"

Mr. Muir's voice was firm, and as Lord Vernham looked at him in surprise, thinking he could not have heard him correctly, there was the sound of the door closing softly as Jarita withdrew from the Salon.

The eyes of the two men met.

"I would like to talk to your daughter."

"There is no need," Mr. Muir replied. "Surely, My Lord, as you are familiar with the East, you are used

to marriages being arranged between the parents of
the bride and groom, or sometimes by an astrologer?"

"We are in England now."

"I have already told you that I consider any meeting
between Jarita and her future husband to be quite unnecessary."

"And if I say they are very necessary?"

"Jarita is under my control until she becomes your
wife, My Lord."

There was no mistaking once again the steel behind
the pleasant words.

Lord Vernham wished to argue, then told himself it
would be wiser to capitulate.

If he had to marry the girl, what did it matter
whether he knew her or not? Whether he liked or disliked her?

As the Bishop had said, the Abbey was worth a
marriage. There was no point of starting an argument
with his future father-in-law, which would not alter by
one iota his decision that, willing or unwilling, two people were to marry each other with what seemed a quite
unnecessary speed.

'If it has to be done,' Lord Vernham thought, 'the
sooner the better and get it over.'

His voice seemed even to himself to be harsh as he
asked:

"What day do you suggest for the ceremony to take
place?"

"Let me see . . ." Mr. Muir replied, "today is Satur-
day. I should imagine the documents can be signed and
the wedding arranged for Thursday."

Lord Vernham was startled, but he was determined
not to show it.

"I am sure that will require a great deal of organisa-
tion on your part," he said with a note of scarcasm in
his voice.

"On the contrary," Mr. Muir answered, "everything
is ready, everything has been planned except the actual

date. So let me say I shall look forward to seeing you,
My Lord, at two o'clock at our Parish Church, pro-
vided of course that your and my Attorneys have approved the business documents that you will take with
you now."

Lord Vernham could not trust himself to reply.

Once again he thought that never in his whole life
had he disliked anyone quite so much as he disliked
his future father-in-law.

*     *     *

Upstairs in a large, beautifully furnished School-
Room which had been redecorated after it ceased to be
a Nursery, Jarita stood trembling.

She had rushed upstairs from the Salon as if she were
being pursued by wild beasts, and she had shut the door
behind her with a bang so that her Governess, seated
sewing by the fireplace, had looked round in surprise.

"What is it, dear?" she asked gently. "And why did
your father want you?"

For a moment Jarita could not reply. Then in a
strange voice which sounded almost as if her teeth
were chattering she said:

"L-Lord . . . V-Vernham was th-there . . . the m-man
I am to m-marry!"

Miss Dawson, the Governess, gave a deep sigh.

"So he has returned home at last. I thought he might
be expected when the Bishop called yesterday."

"He is very t-tall and b-big," Jarita said, "a m-mon-
ster of a m-man!"

"Now, Jarita, do not frighten yourself. I am sure he
is very pleasant. I have heard him very well spoken of."

Jarita did not reply, but merely went to the window
to curl up on the windowseat and stare into the garden.

She was thinking how large and overpowering Lord
Vernham had looked and she knew she was as fright-

ened of him as she had been of Gervaise Verne, whom her father told her she must marry.

"I cannot do it . . . I cannot!" she said beneath her breath.

"What did you say, dearest?" Miss Dawson asked.

Jarita did not repeat the words. She was thinking desperately and frantically of a plan that had been forming in her mind ever since she had learnt that Gervaise was dead and that his cousin had been sent for from some strange, outlandish place on the other side of the world.

Not that her father had told her any of these things. In fact he never told her anything except to give her orders, which she obeyed immediately because she knew the consequences if she did not.

But the servants in the house talked, and because most of them had been there ever since she was a child they often behaved in the casual manner of adults as if she were deaf.

She had learnt a great deal about Gervaise Verne, not only from what the Housekeeper said to Miss Dawson and the gossip that was continually exchanged amongst the housemaids, but also from Emma.

This was her own personal maid, who was a young, apple-cheeked girl from the village of Little Kingsclere.

Emma had been promoted from housemaid at Miss Dawson's suggestion, to look exclusively after Jarita.

Jarita knew it was because her Governess, who loved her and really cared about her well-being, had felt it unnatural that she should be brought up without the companionship of girls of her own age.

"I suggested to your father that you should share your lessons with some of the girls in the neighbour-hood," she had told Jarita often enough. "I would like you to have parties here and perhaps in the winter you could dance and in the summer play games on the lawn."

"Papa will not let me do anything except prepare

myself for the position I am to hold one day as a Lady of Title," Jarita answered.

"I know, dearest," Miss Dawson sighed, "and although I begged him to be a little more lenient with you, he will not listen."

Jarita had often wondered how she could have endured her existence after her mother died if Miss Dawson had not been there.

She had loved her sweet, understanding mother with an adoration that a child will give when she has no-one else but a parent on whom to expend her affection.

Mrs. Muir had never been in good health.

As Lord Vernham was to learn later, she came from an aristocratic family in the North and was one of five daughters. Although her father had not been particularly impressed by Theobold Muir, he had given his consent to the marriage because he was such a wealthy man.

Jarita had realised when she was still very young that her mother was frightened of her father.

He always seemed courteous and considerate where she was concerned.

But being so much on her own, she had developed her sensitivities more than was usual in a girl of her age and she knew that her parents had little affection for each other.

Her father was often absent for long periods, journeying South on business, or visiting towns where he owned property, but it always seemed to her that as soon as he was away the house seemed lighter and gayer and the sun shone.

Her mother would laugh and be quite a different person than when her father was at home.

Then, quite unexpectedly and with very little warning, her mother died, and to Jarita it seemed as if the light went out of her life.

After that her father seemed to become almost

fanatical in planning her education for every second of
the day.

There was not only Miss Dawson, who soon was
relegated very much into the background; there were
teachers on every subject who were brought in car-
riages drawn by swift horses from every part of the
Country.

To Jarita the subjects in which she had to be pro-
ficient were endless.

She began to realise that just as her father demanded
perfection round him, he also wanted perfection in his
only child.

"If you had been a boy," he said to Jarita once,
"I would have set you up in business and taught you
how to carry on the projects in which I have been so
successful. But because you are a girl you will have
to shine in another sphere."

"And where is that, Papa?" Jarita asked innocently.

"You will be a social figure," her father said firmly.
"You will be joined by marriage to one of the oldest
and most distinguished families in the land. You will
have a title that everyone will respect."

"How is this possible?" Jarita asked, bewildered.

Her father had smiled before he replied, almost as
if he spoke to himself:

"You will have a fortune, my dear, which few men
would find themselves able to refuse."

It was only when Jarita thought this over that she
realised exactly what it portended.

She was to be sold, as if she were a piece of
merchandise, to a man who required her money, just
as her father desired his title.

It was not hard for her to guess that the husband
her father desired for her lived next door.

Ever since she could understand what people said,
she had heard her father talking of the magnificence
of Vernham Abbey, of its ancient origin, and of the

Vernes themselves, who figured in the history-books which she read with one of her teachers.

"Your father is very ambitious, dearest," her mother said to her once. "He always wants what is out of reach; he always determines to possess the unobtainable."

But Vernham Abbey in fact was not unobtainable, as Jarita had learnt not from her father but from Emma.

"His Lorship's been here ag'in today," Emma would relate as she arranged Jarita's hair.

"Lord Vernham?"

"Yes. Arrives down from London, he did, last night, me brother tells me. He has a look round the Abbey and comes over here first thing this morning."

Emma would lower her voice and look over her shoulder.

"They're a-bettin' in the servants' Hall, Miss Jarita, as how there'll be some more pictures in Aladdin's Cave a-fore the week's out."

Aladdin's Cave was the way the servants referred to the huge store packed with things which had come from the Abbey.

Once or twice when her father had been away from home, Jarita had persuaded the Groom of the Chambers, who had the key, to let her look inside.

He was an old man devoted to Jarita ever since she had been able to toddle towards him, fascinated by his livery with its brightly coloured buttons.

"Only a peep now, Miss Jarita," he said. "You'll get me into trouble, you will."

"You know I would never tell Papa," Jarita answered. "What is new, Groomy?"

It was a pet name she had given him and one of which he was very proud.

"Some pieces of silver, Miss Jarita, and a picture of goddesses and cupids. Very pretty—but it'll be better when it's been cleaned."

"Oh, let me see! Let me see," Jarita begged.

Because he found it hard to refuse, Groomy would show her the pictures, the silver, and sometimes, if he was in a very good mood, let her handle the gold snuff-boxes set with enamel and diamonds.

He would also sometimes open one of the cabinets in which there were exquisite figures in Dresden China, which delighted her more than anything else.

It was only when she learnt that she was to marry Gervaise Verne that Jarita no longer wished to visit Aladdin's Cave and knew what it was to be really afraid.

She had always been afraid of her father, but this was different.

It was Emma who told her about Gervaise's behaviour with the girls in the village and at first Jarita had not understood what she meant.

"Betsy went and killed herself last night, Miss. She were a relative o' mine," Emma said, her eyes red with weeping.

"Why should she do such a terrible thing?" Jarita asked.

For a moment Emma could not reply.

"Tell me . . . please tell me," Jarita begged.

"It's that Mr. Gervaise Verne—real wicked he is! Never leaving Betsy alone, though she tried to keep him away from her."

"Why would he not leave her alone?"

"He was after her, Miss Jarita, and we all warns her wot he intended, but then she becomes fascinated by him."

Jarita found it hard to understand what had happened.

She had never seen Gervaise Verne, but she knew from her father how important the Vernes were and it seemed strange that he should seek the company of a village girl.

"He gets her to meet him in the Park night after

night when he were down here," Emma went on, tears
running down her cheeks, "and 'though her mother and
father tried to put a stop to it, they were aliving in a
cottage belonging to His Lordship and were afraid
they'd be chucked out."

"Are you saying that Betsy was in love with Mr.
Gervaise?" Jarita asked.

"If yer calls that love, Miss. There's nastier names
for it. Bad an' wicked he is, and Betsy not yet seven-
teen and a bit stupid-like, as you might say, for all she
was the prettiest girl in the village. Now she's gorn
and killed herself!"

"But how? And why?"

"Throws herself in the whirlpool, Miss. They fishes
her body out this morning."

The whirlpool!

Jarita knew it well. There was a place in the river
below where the Monks had widened it into a lake
where there was a cascade, and for some reason at
the foot of it there was a whirlpool.

Every village child was warned to keep away, and it
was well-known that once one got into the whirlpool
there was no chance of ever getting out.

"Why did she kill herself?" Jarita persisted.

Emma had looked over her shoulder to be quite
certain no-one could overhear her, then she whispered:

"She were havin' a baby, Miss Jarita! Mr. Gervaise's
child! They're sayin' he wouldn't acknowledge it and
refused to help Betsy in any way!"

It was no wonder that, having heard this, and other
stories of Gervaise Verne's behaviour, when she was
informed by her father that she was to marry him Jarita
had protested violently.

"No, no, Papa! Not Gervaise Verne! I could not
marry him! He is bad and wicked!"

"How can you know? Who has been talking to you?"

The question was sharp, and instantly Jarita realized
she must protect Emma or she would be dismissed.

"I heard . . . people . . . t-talking about him when
I was in the . . . village, Papa," she answered.

"What were you doing in the village?"

"I was buying something at the shop."

"I cannot believe there is anything of importance
for you to buy in Little Kingsclere," Mr. Muir had
said coldly. "In future, you will do your shopping
elsewhere."

"It does not matter where I shop, Papa, but I have
no wish to marry Gervaise Verne."

"You will marry whom I tell you to marry," her
father had replied. "When his father dies he will become Lord Vernham. You will live at the Abbey and
I shall be proud! Do you hear me, Jarita? Proud to
know that my daughter is the mistress of one of the
most famous houses in England."

Jarita had thought that a house, however beautiful,
was hardly compensation for a cruel and wicked husband, but while she struggled for words her father said
curtly:

"I will hear no more of this nonsense. You are not
capable of choosing a husband for yourself. You will
marry whom I tell you to marry, and there will be no
argument about it!"

A thousand protests rose to Jarita's lips but she dared
not express them. Instead with her usual meekness she
answered:

"Yes . . . Papa."

Then she had run upstairs to find Emma and tell
her in tones of horror what had occurred.

"I am to . . . marry Mr. Gervaise Verne! Oh . . .
Emma . . . Emma . . . what am I to do?"

If Jarita was stricken by the idea, so was Emma,
all the more because she realised it was her own in-
discreet tongue which had made things worse for her
beloved young mistress than they might otherwise have
been

Too late she realized that in her ignorance she had

not thought of Miss Jarita as being old enough to be married, and certainly not to a man who was loathed and despised by everyone in the village of Little Kingsclere.

"I'm sure he'll treat yer right, Miss," she tried to say consolingly. "After all, you're a lady. Perhaps he's only bad when he's dealing with the likes o' us."

"But . . . Betsy . . ." Jarita managed to say, "and little . . . Mary . . ."

She could hardly articulate the last word and though both girls knew what the other was thinking they could not bear to speak of it.

It was Emma who rejoiced quite unashamedly when it was learnt that Gervaise Verne was dead.

"I've the best bit o' news I could ever give yer, Miss," she had cried, bursting into Jarita's bed-room.

"What is?" Jarita asked sleepily.

"Mr. Gervaise Verne, Miss. He's dead!"

"Dead?" Jarita exclaimed, sitting up in bed. "How can he be?"

"Killed in an accident, Miss, and His Lordship with him. You can't marry him now, that's for sure!"

"Oh . . . Emma . . . is it true . . . is it really true?"

"Everyone downstairs is talking about it, Miss, and they've told the master."

Jarita was therefore prepared when her father sent for her.

"It is with deep regret, Jarita," he said, "that I have to inform you that your fiancé, Gervaise Verne, has been killed in an accident."

"That must be a tragedy for his family, Papa," Jarita said in a composed voice.

"His father was killed, too."

Jarita had the feeling, although she could not be sure, that her father was not very perturbed that his so-called friend had died.

There was silence and after a moment hesitatingly she asked:

"Who . . . will live at the . . . Abbey now . . .
Papa?"

"I am not quite certain," her father answered, "but
I intend to find out."

In his usual strangely enigmatic manner he had not
spoken of the matter again to her.

But some months later Emma learnt that the new
Lord Vernham was somewhere in Africa and a letter
had been sent to inform him that he had inherited the
title.

"Do you think he is already married?" Jarita had
asked Emma.

"No-one knows, Miss. They've not heard from Mr.
Alvaric for years, not since he went off to them foreign
parts."

"Why did he go?"

"His father was killed at Waterloo and I've always
heard, 'though of course I was just a child at the time,
that Mr. Alvaric never got on with Mr. Gervaise. Always fightin' they was, as boys."

Jarita felt she could understand that. At the same
time, the knowledge that there was a new Lord Vernham began to overshadow her thoughts and the feeling
of freedom she had enjoyed since Gervaise Verne's
death.

She sensed that her father was awaiting his return
with an eagerness he would not admit.

People continually came and went in Aladdin's
Cave and she knew that in the Estate Office her father
was drawing up new plans and that two new clerks
had been employed to work on them.

It was only one day when she went into the Office
to fetch something she required that she glanced down
on one of the desks and saw a blueprint which bore
the words: "Vernham Abbey Estate."

It was then that the feeling that she was travelling
towards a strange and frightening destination began to
creep over her.

The point of impact was coming nearer and she knew nothing she could say or do would prevent it from reaching her.

Now sitting in the window of her Sitting-Room she knew the impact had been made.

She could see again all too clearly, though she had not raised her eyes, the tall, broad-shouldered figure of Lord Vernham with his arm outstretched towards the grog-tray.

He was taller than her father and had seemed immense and at the same time dark and ominous.

It had only been a fleeting glance, before keeping her eyes downcast for the rest of the time she was in the Salon.

But it had been enough, she thought, enough to know that as this man was another Verne she could rather die than marry him.

"What are you thinking of, dearest?" Miss Dawson asked. "Come and share your thoughts with me. You know things always seem better when one talks them over."

It was something they had done together ever since Miss Dawson had taken charge of her, but in this instance Jarita knew there could be no confidences because that would involve the person she loved better than anyone else in the house.

What she was thinking must remain a secret, so secret that no-one in any circumstances must guess what it was.

With an effort she rose from the window-seat and walked towards her Governess.

"You know I do not wish to be married," she said, "mostly because I cannot bear to leave you, Dawsie. You have been so kind to me since Mama died."

She knelt beside Miss Dawson's chair and put her head against her breast.

"I hate to leave you, too, dearest," Miss Dawson said,

dropping her sewing and putting her arms round Jarita.

She held her close, then said:

"Perhaps in a year or so, who knows, I might be able to come back to you."

"How could you do that?" Jarita asked in a muffled voice.

"When you have children, dearest, you would want them to have lessons and be as clever as you are. I could teach them just as I taught you."

Jarita moved a little closer to her.

At the same time, inside her a voice was saying:

"Children with that man? Never! Never! Never!"

# Chapter Three

Jarita rose before dawn to move softly about her bedroom.

She had not been able to sleep, but had lain listening to the quietness of the house, feeling that even the silence was ominous and a threat which made her tremble.

She knew that Miss Dawson would now be fast asleep in her room on the other side of the passage and the housemaids would not yet be stirring. Even the horses would be shut up and silent in the stables.

She had tried to think during the night how she could ride away from her home, but she had known that it would be impossible for her to saddle a horse and take it from its stable without arousing one of the grooms who slept in the lofts over the stalls.

She decided therefore she must walk, and although she had no idea what her destination would be, she was sure she would find a village or a small town where she could get lodgings and where she could be anonymous.

It was all very vague in her mind because Jarita, having been looked after and cosseted all her life, had really no notion how she could fend for herself.

The first thing she required was money. This was the most difficult problem of all, because when she went shopping Miss Dawson always paid for everything.

Jarita looked in her purse and found she had several half-sovereigns, for putting in the offertory bag when she attended a service in the Parish Church.

This, she was well aware, would not last long, but she had a considerable amount of jewellery.

Her own possessions were mostly childish bangles and brooches in gold set with pearls and semi-precious stones, but she also had in her jewel case two brooches which had belonged to her mother and a bracelet.

Mrs. Muir's valuable jewellery, which included some magnificent pieces, was all kept in the safe in the Pantry and was therefore, as far as Jarita was concerned, unobtainable.

She was however quite sure that her mother's brooches would fetch a considerable sum.

Her father had never bought his wife anything but the very best, and although she knew only a little about stones Jarita was aware that these were blue-white diamonds and the large centrepiece in each brooch was valuable.

The bracelet, too, which she had worn for sentimental reasons, was a period-piece and the diamonds glistened brightly as she took them from their velvet bed.

She rolled all her jewellery up in handkerchiefs and placed them on a small white shawl in which she intended to convey all she could take with her.

She was well aware that it would be impossible for her to walk for long carrying anything heavy.

She therefore added to the jewels only one night-gown, a change of under-clothing, a brush and a comb, and a tooth-brush.

Even those, she thought, might prove wearisome if she had to walk far.

She then chose from her wardrobe the plainest of her gowns, which was dark in colour.

As it was the beginning of summer all her winter clothes had been taken away by Emma to be cleaned, pressed, and put away in another wardrobe until they were required again at the end of September.

But there was one gown, a dark blue silk which Jarita had worn on colder mornings, and this she put on.

She had a little trouble in fastening the buttons at the back of the neck because she was not used to dressing herself, then she decided that to be practical she must take a cloak with her in case it rained.

There was in fact a cloak which matched the gown, but the bonnet she normally wore with it was trimmed with small ostrich feathers and she felt certain this would look far too striking for a young girl travelling alone.

She therefore placed a soft scarf over her head and hoped thus not to attract attention.

By the time she was dressed the dawn had not yet come, although the sky had lightened. Looking out the window, she was able to see across the garden and distinguish the statues and urns which stood against the shrubs.

This was the time, Jarita thought, when she must leave, and picking up her bundle she had a last glance round her bed-room, feeling she was leaving behind her childhood and so many happy memories of her mother.

Then the thought that she would be leaving this room anyway in a few days to marry the huge dark monster of a man whom she had seen in the Salon made her hastily pull open the door and start to tiptoe down the passage.

*   *   *

It was three hours later when the sun was growing warm that Jarita took off her cloak and put it over her arm.

She felt she had walked a long way since leaving Kingsclere House, but it had in fact been tiring not so much because of the distance she had covered as because she had taken to the fields.

She had reasoned that when she was found to be missing her father would doubtless set out to look for her driving his Curricle. That meant that he would keep to the roads.

If she intended to hide herself, therefore, she knew it would be far safer to make her way across country.

She had soon left behind the Park-land which surrounded her home, and skirting the village in case she should be seen she crossed some grass fields, then came to a number that were sown.

This meant that she had to make detours round them and because she regretted the delay involved she walked as quickly as she could, but found it hardgoing.

She had unfortunately found no winter shoes in her wardrobe but only the soft kid slippers that she wore in the summer.

Stones, pieces of wood, and the rough turf on which she walked were at times painful to her feet, and once or twice she had to sit down and shake out fine soil or small stones from her slippers.

It was now that she began to feel hungry and thought she had been very remiss in not bringing with her something to eat, or perhaps by leaving through the kitchens eating something first.

She had been so agitated last night that she had hardly touched any dinner and now with the unwonted exercise she began to feel empty inside.

She wondered if it would be possible to buy a bun or something to eat in a village shop, and she remembered hearing vaguely that travellers could obtain bread and cheese at a public house.

Then she told herself she was still far too near to Kingsclere.

Even though she was plainly dressed she would nevertheless be an object of curiosity for the yokels in any village, who would doubtless later, if her father or his servants made enquiries, report that she had been seen.

She therefore hurried on and as she had anticipated her bundle seemed to grow heavier and even the effort of carrying her cloak made her feel hot.

She undid her chiffon scarf and took it from her head, knowing the sun would not be strong enough at this time of the year to give her sunstroke, a complaint that Miss Dawson had often warned her against.

She passed through a small wood, little more than a copse, which was cool and shady. But the rains of two or three days ago had made the twisting path damp and muddy and Jarita found her slippers slipped in the wet.

Then there were more fields, until in the distance she saw the spire of a Church and the roofs of some houses clustering round it.

She thought she knew what the village was called and was aware she was travelling north as she had intended.

But it would have been far too dangerous to be seen and again she made a detour.

Occasionally in the distance she saw men working in the fields but the moment she spotted them she moved quickly out of their sight.

She actually encountered no-one who might have spoken to her.

She walked on steadily, and now the sun seemed to become hotter and hotter and she was not only hungry but thirsty.

"I shall have to stop sooner or later," she decided.

She crossed the main highway and climbed over a

stile into a grass field where a small flock of sheep were grazing at one side of it.

Jarita walked straight across the middle to where at the far end she could see trees.

"When I reach the shelter of them," she told herself, "I will sit down and rest. Afterwards I must walk on until I can find some food."

She was halfway across the field when looking back she saw a carriage passing along the roadway.

Her heart gave a sudden leap of fear as she thought it might be her father, but it passed on, and when she looked back again there was only a man on horseback who seemed to be looking towards her.

Then she told herself she was imagining it, and in fact when she glanced back again he had turned round and ridden away in the direction from which he had come.

It was not far now to the safety of the trees and Jarita with an effort started to walk so much faster that she was almost running.

She had nearly reached them when she heard the sound of a horse's hoofs behind her and looked over her shoulder.

Now there was no mistaking who was approaching and with a little gasp of terror she dropped her cloak and started to run frantically towards the wood.

She had however only gone a few yards before she heard the horse just behind her and she felt the whiplash of a riding-crop strike her across the shoulders.

She gave a little scream of sheer terror and fell down.

As she looked up at her father towering above her, the expression on his face told her that he was in one of his rages that she had feared ever since she was a child.

But now she thought despairingly he was angrier than she had ever seen him.

"Get up!"

The order rang out like a pistol-shot, and feeling as if her legs would hardly carry her Jarita struggled to her feet, leaving her small bundle on the ground as she did so.

"Give that to me!"

Her father pointed towards it, and obediently, feeling as if her will had gone and it was impossible even to think clearly, Jarita picked up the bundle and held it up to him.

He took it from her, opened it, and saw what it contained.

He put her money and the handkerchiefs containing her jewellery in the pocket of his coat, then disdainfully he threw the shawl containing her nightgown and other garments onto the ground.

"Walk!" he commanded.

She stared up at him for a moment, finding it hard even to understand what he told her to do.

Then as she appeared to hesitate he once again lashed her with his riding-crop. It cut across her shoulders, making her give a scream of fear like an animal caught in a trap.

Afterwards Jarita could never remember that nightmare return to her home.

Her father forced her to walk ahead of him and several times when she faltered or fell down he struck her again.

Once when she felt she had no longer the strength to move she cried piteously:

"I cannot do it, Papa! I cannot go any further!"

"You walked here, and you will walk back!" he said grimly, and whipped her until she rose.

When finally they reached the drive at Kingsclere she was moving so slowly that her father's horse had come almost to a standstill.

Jarita saw the house through a haze of exhaustion so that it appeared to move dizzily in the distance almost as if it were a mirage.

Somehow by a superhuman effort she reached the front-door steps.

As she climbed up them she put out her hands beseechingly towards Groomby, who was standing just inside the Hall, but he had one glance at his master and knew that he dared not help her.

Theobold Muir dismounted from his horse and walked into the Hall behind Jarita.

"Go to my Study!"

She could hardy remember where it was.

Everything seemed to be very dark and she felt as if she was walking through a fog. She could no longer think and could only feel the pain her father had inflicted upon her.

A footman opened the door of the Study and she staggered into it.

She reached the centre of the room and put up a trembling hand to push back her hair from her forehead, knowing it was untidy and falling round her face.

She thought she should go upstairs and make herself presentable, when she heard the door of the Study close and turned round slowly.

Her father had come into the room and was walking towards her.

She took one glance at his face, contorted with anger, at the long thin whip which he held in his hand, and started to scream. . . .

* * *

Lord Vernham awoke with the uncomfortable feeling that something unpleasant was about to happen. Then he remembered that it was his wedding-day.

He had, although he had not expected to, slept deeply and dreamlessly simply because he was tired out.

There had been so much to do these last four days that he had never seemed to have a moment to himself.

The day after he had visited Theobold Muir his Attorneys had arrived first thing in the morning and the marriage settlement had been set out for his approval together with a surprising number of plans for the restoration of the Abbey and the Estate.

They made Lord Vernham square his chin and his mouth tightened as he realised these had been prepared a long time ago and covered everything that might be required on the whole property.

It was all very efficient and the suggestions were in fact overwhelmingly generous considering who was paying for them.

At the same time, he could not help feeling it was intolerable that he must rely on a stranger to restore the house of his forefathers, to repair the farms, and to bring the land back to fertility.

There was however nothing he could do but accept the situation and try to do so with dignity, without letting the Solicitors and Clerks be aware of the resentment he felt inside him.

With regard to the Abbey itself, he was aware that the proposed renovations were in perfect good taste and in fact Theobold Muir had merely planned restoring it to what it had been at the time of the Ninth Lord Vernham, who had been Alvaric's grandfather.

There was no doubt that Mr. Muir had done the most careful research.

The patterns of the curtains he suggested for every room were pinned beside the designs for the room itself and in almost every case they were a replica of the curtains which originally hung there.

The only difference was that the new materials were a better quality and therefore far more expensive.

Everything had been measured up and designed to scale.

As Lord Vernham turned over plan after plan and the men who had drawn them explained what was intended, it was hard for him to resist tearing them

into small pieces and shouting that he would rather
live in the house as it was than be beholden to such a
benefactor.

But the self-control he had exercised all his life prevented him from showing any sign of the tempest he
felt.

Instead he passed the plans without making a single
alteration, then dismissed the Solicitors and Clerks
with a courtesy they appreciated.

"When do you intend to start?" he asked when they
were actually on the door-step.

"Mr. Muir's instructions were that, with Your
Lordship's permission, sixty carpenters, painters, stone-
masons, and gilders should enter the Abbey at two
o'clock on Thursday."

Lord Vernham was tense as he realised this was the
exact moment at which he was due at the Church to
be married.

"They will camp in the grounds or in the attics,"
one of the designers explained, "and they will work
from dawn until dusk until the work is completed."

"Thank you."

The words were spoken with an effort.

As they drove away Lord Vernham went back into
the Hall to stand looking at the emptiness of it, at the
damp, streaked walls, the broken panes of glass in the
long windows, and the marks where the tapestries and
pictures had once hung.

Then he gave a deep sigh and tried to forget everything but the fact that he had to prepare for his
animals, who would be arriving, he hoped, before the
actual day of the wedding.

He had arranged that the South Wing of the Abbey,
where the Master Bed-Rooms were situated should be
left to the last.

Here was the huge room which his grandfather had
always used and opening out of it was another room,

equally impressive and perhaps more attractive, which had been his grandmother's.

The huge canopied beds had been unsalable and had therefore remained in the places for which they had been designed many centuries ago.

The furniture was sparse since all the valuable tables, commodes, and chairs had long since been sold by his his uncle to Theobold Muir.

But by collecting almost every remaining piece of furniture from the other rooms the two bed-rooms did not look too empty, even though Lord Vernham was quite sure there was not the luxury to which his future wife had been accustomed.

He could not help feeling with a twist to his lips that it would do her good to rough it for a little.

Then he wondered how she would manage if she ever had to live as he had in a tent in the desert, a straw hut in a native village, or even spend the night with no other shelter but a tree in the jungle.

He knew when he thought about Jarita that he was afraid she might be like her father and he would dislike her on sight as he had disliked Mr. Muir.

It had been impossible to judge what she was like with just a glimpse of a bent head, a white forehead, and a slim figure.

But he told himself that if she tried to boss him or behave in an autocratic manner as her father was doing he would stand up to her from the very beginning and make quite certain who was master of the Abbey.

The thought that perhaps there might be wordy battle with the woman who would oppose him simply because it was her money that he was forced to spend made Lord Vernham feel rebellious in a manner that was a strain on his self-control.

Only by physical exercise could he force himself to forget the difficulties which might lie ahead and concentrate on the immediate needs of his animals, which should be getting nearer to him every day.

He went down to the village and found, as he had expected, that many of the old retainers who had served the Estate in his grandfather's time had either been dismissed or left because they were paid no wages by his uncle.

They were almost pathetically eager to come back, and because he wanted so much to have his own people round him Lord Vernham even engaged those who he was well aware were past being of very much use.

Nevertheless, there was quite a number of years of useful service left in the man who had been the Head-gardener, and in several of those who had worked under him.

The younger men had been little more than youths when he was a boy, but they had helped the game-keepers and the foresters, and they too were eager to return.

He had a large number of willing hands eventually to help him erect the fences which were to enclose first a place for his lions, then one for the cheetahs.

He had to explain exactly what he required and several men were sent off to the timber-yard to buy the required fencing, others to get nails, and it was only midday on Monday that they finally started working.

"Why did ye bring these savage animals with ye, Master Alvaric?" asked an old man called Ryman, who had been a forester in the past.

"They are not savage as far as I am concerned," Lord Vernham replied. "I have had the lions with me ever since they were cubs and they are as gentle as any cat might be, while the cheetahs have been trained to hunt."

"To hunt, Master Alvaric? How be that possible?" Lord Vernham smiled.

"Cheetahs have been more or less domesticated in Asia for centuries."

The old man had looked interested and he continued:

"They can run faster than any animal in the world, in fact it has been estimated that a cheetah can run twice as fast as a race-horse!"

There was an expression of astonishment on the faces of every man listening and Lord Vernham explained:

"Cheetahs and leopards were used by the nobility in England for coursing until about a century ago, and there are many pictures of them being carried on horse-back behind the saddle."

Lord Vernham smiled as he added:

"The history-books tell us this is what happened in the time of Kublai Khan, but I think we should have to train a modern horse not to be terrified if after a kill a cheetah were to leap onto his haunches!"

"That be true enough!" old Ryman said. "And wot would this strange animal be a-huntin' here?"

"Hares are the usual quarry, but of course in their native state any kind of deer or goat is a natural prey."

As he spoke Lord Vernham glanced to where in the Park there were a few spotted deer left from the big herd that he could remember in the past.

The hinds had given birth to a number of small gazelle-like little kids that were trying to struggle along on spindly legs.

"I want you to make it impossible for the cheetahs to get out of the enclosure," he said. "Remember, they can climb to the top of a tree and up a high fence unless we make it too difficult for them to scramble over it."

He showed the men how this could be done, then supervised the village carpenters as they made a comfortable flat-topped house for the lions.

"They will sit on the top looking out," he told the men. "Any wild animal likes to survey the land round him."

He realised that his workmen were all extremely
surprised at the care he took and the comfort he
required for his animals.

The enclosures were very large so that they would
not feel constrained, and when Lord Vernham took off
his coat to work beside those driving the posts into
the ground they stared at him.

Only the older ones, like Ryman, chuckled to themselves.

"Yer Lordship 'asn't altered much," one of them
said. "Ye were just the same as a boy. Always ready
to help and not too grand to get yer hands dirty."

"I hope I shall never be that," Lord Verham smiled.

When later he had stood them pints of beer and
cider in the small pub which had not altered in the
last hundred years, they cheered him.

But today there was no chance of his working and
he thought with a scowl that the hours would pass
slowly until it was time to be at the village Church.

He had supposed as there had been so much haste
about the wedding that it would be a very quiet affair,
but he learnt from the number of notes that had been
brought to him in the last two days that everyone of
importance in the County had been invited.

The notes had welcomed him back as his father's
son, and he realised more from what they left unsaid
than from what had been written that they were not
surprised that he was to marry Theobold Muir's daughter.

It gave Lord Vernham a feeling that he was being
manipulated, forced down a path that was not of his
own choosing, well-trod and skilfully prepared so there
could be no deviation from it.

"I have never felt so damned frustrated in the whole
of my life!" he told himself beneath his breath.

His father's valet, whom he had found still living
in the village, had come back to serve him, and
Holden had already laid out his wedding-garments and

several new muslin cravats which had been hastily purchased in St. Albans.

Lord Vernham looked at them with distaste, then shrugging himself into his old clothes went down the stairs to breakfast.

There was only a table, two chairs, and a side-board in the small Dining-Room that he had decided to use while the Baronial Hall was being set in order.

The chairs did not match and the back of one of them was broken, which was the reason, he thought, why his uncle had not sold it to Theobold Muir.

The linen cloth on the table was spotlessly clean but it was darned in several places, and the china was a mixture: cups from one service, plates from another, and there was obviously no silver-dish for the eggs and bacon which were waiting for him.

Holden served him, saying apologetically:

"I'm afraid, M'Lord, there's not the variety I would wish to offer Your Lordship, but I understands there's horses coming into the stables this afternoon and grooms who can go shopping for what we shall require tomorrow."

Lord Vernham did not reply.

He had already learnt from his future father-in-law that a number of horses from the Kingsclere stables were to be despatched to the Abbey for his use until he could purchase his own.

Although he could have obtained credit, some fastidiousness in him prevented him from running up debts until he had actually paid for his wife's money by handing her his coronet.

"It is all I require, thank you, Holden," he said curtly.

"I has a feeling, M'Lord, that the animals you're expecting will be here at any moment."

Lord Vernham sat up with a different expression on his face.

"What do you mean?"

"Young Bill, one of the wood-cutters's sons, came into the kitchen, M'Lord, a few minutes ago and said there were three big wagons in the village asking the way to the Abbey."

"They have arrived, Holden! That is splendid!" Lord Vernham exclaimed.

He ate the last piece of bacon on his plate, then rising from the table walked quickly towards the front of the house.

From there he could look over the stone bridge which spanned the end of the lake and up the long drive with its ancient oak trees towards where the Park-land bordered the high road.

He stood for some seconds waiting, then coming slowly down the drive he saw the four heavy cart-horses dragging on an open dray one of the huge cages which contained his animals.

"Here they come, Holden!" he said, and it was impossible to keep the excitement out of his voice.

*　*　*

There was however a very different expression on Lord Vernham's face when he sat beside his bride in the Dining-Room at Kingsclere.

After the ceremony in the Church when the packed congregation had seemed to him to be a crowd of nothing but unfamiliar faces and curious eyes, he found in fact a great number of old friends whom he had half-forgotten in the years he had been abroad.

Now almost despite himself he was delighted to see them, and the warm manner in which they spoke of his father and the welcome they gave him were extremely heartening.

"It is delightful to think of you back at the Abbey," everybody seemed to be saying in one way or another until Lord Vernham could not help responding with an enthusiasm which echoed that of those who shook his hand so fervently.

As the Wedding Breakfast, which was as might have been expected an epicurean feast, began, His Lordship realised that he had not been able yet to speak a single word to his wife.

In the Church her face had not only been veiled as she had come up the aisle on her father's arm, but she kept her head bowed in the same manner as when he had first met her.

He had in fact been a little startled when he had taken her hand in his to place the ring on her finger to find it was icily cold despite the fact that it was a very warm day.

He was himself feeling uncomfortably hot because he had spent the morning getting his animals into their enclosures, and it had taken so long that he had to change in a considerable hurry to reach the Church on time.

It was fortunate, he thought, as he waited at the altar-steps, that Holden had not lost his cunning when it came to tying a cravat, and he hoped that he did not look anything but aristocratic.

At the same time, he was very conscious from the hard work he had undertaken these last few days that his finger-nails were split and the skin on his hands had hardened in a manner of which most noblemen would have been extremely ashamed.

What had pleased him more than anything else was that his cheetahs had survived the journey and appeared in excellent health, and that even his lioness, Bella, who had recently given birth to cubs, had not seemed particularly disturbed.

They had all shown their delight at seeing him, too, and the parrots had been released from the small cages in which they had travelled into the Orangery, where he had put what shrubs and ferns he could find to make it seem more like home.

The interest of it had prevented him from brooding over what lay ahead.

Only as he repeated the solemn vows of the Marriage Service did Lord Vernham feel once again a sense of rebellion rising within him because he was being forced into doing something contrary to every instinct in his body.

His Uncle Lorimer, the Bishop of Axminster, had married them, and as if he knew what his nephew was feeling, when they reached the Reception at Kingsclere House he had said in a quiet voice that no-one else could hear:

"I am very proud of you, Alvaric, and I know if your father was alive he would say the same thing."

It had been impossible not to smile, but it was difficult to continue to do so when Theobold Muir rose to propose the toast to the bride and groom. He made a well-phrased but at the same time boastful speech which made Lord Vernham feel uncomfortable.

These were minor irritations, however, and knowing it was expected he turned to speak to his wife, only to find that she would answer him in nothing but monosyllables and that she never once raised her eyes.

He visualised himself enduring years of this and wondered how he could possibly live with it.

Then he told himself that she was obviously very young and shy and perhaps when they were alone together things would be easier.

There was naturally no chance of any sort of conversation.

After the ceremony they had received the guests for nearly two hours and the Wedding Breakfast with its myriad courses and its speeches accounted for another three.

It was therefore eight o'clock when finally it was time for the bride and bridegroom to leave Kingsclere House for Vernham Abbey.

It was only a question of driving two miles, but

this entailed passing through the village and Lord Vernham was surprised to find that the celebrations there were far more elaborate than he had expected.

There were not only arches of welcome and fluttering flags across the road, but also the whole population of Little Kingsclere was lining their route, and fireworks were let off on the village green as soon as they appeared.

Lord Vernham wondered if they had been paid for by the villagers themselves or whether they were another provision by his father-in-law.

He felt it would be unwise to ask such a question, and when the carriage stopped he merely rose and made another speech of thanks and appreciation on behalf of his wife and himself.

The cheers were spontaneous and the good wishes very sincere.

As they were showered with flower petals and rice, the open carriage in which they were travelling seemed also filled with good will as the horses turned in at the gates of the Abbey.

As soon as they moved beneath the trees Lord Vernham could see the great building in the distance ablaze with lights.

He had grown used since he had come home to seeing it dark and lifeless at the end of the day, but now every window seemed to blaze forth a welcome.

At first he was surprised, then he realized that just as had been promised the workmen had moved in and taken over the house at the very moment he had placed the ring on Jarita's finger and made her his wife.

"I am afraid we are going to find it very noisy," he said. "Your father has already started his plans of restoration and I am only hoping that the South Wing, where we are sleeping, will prove almost sound-proof."

She did not reply, but raised her head for a moment to look at the Abbey towards which they were advancing.

She was still wearing her wedding-gown and although the veil had been swept back over the huge diamond tiara she wore in her hair, it still fell like a curtain on either side of her face.

"I do not know if you have ever visited my house before," Lord Vernham went on, "but it is full of history and I shall look forward to telling you some of the stories of the past about my ancestors who lived here."

He thought that she shivered but he could not be sure, and although he expected a reply he did not receive one as the horses drew up outside the Abbey door.

Now there was not only Holden to meet them but a number of tall young footmen wearing the Verne livery, which Lord Vernham supposed must have been something else which his uncle had sold to Theobold Muir.

The crested buttons alone were valuable simply because many of them had been made in the reign of George I, but he had forgotten how smart and distinguished flunkeys could look in their powdered wigs and that the Groom of the Chambers' uniform was so resplendent.

A footman opened the door of the carriage and Lord Vernham stepped out.

He offered his hand to Jarita and once again he was surprised at how cold her fingers were as they trembled in his.

For the first time he felt rather sorry for her. This must, he thought, be a considerable ordeal.

"Welcome, M'Lord and M'Lady!" the Groom of the Chambers said pompously. "The staff desire me to convey on their behalf our wishes for Your Lordship's and Ladyship's happiness and a long life in the future."

"Thank you," Lord Vernham replied, hoping they did not expect him to make a third speech.

As he entered the Hall there was a long line of

servants lined up to shake hands with him and Jarita, and to his relief he found that quite a number of them were those he had engaged himself.

For one terrifying moment he had thought his father-in-law had restocked the Abbey to the point where there would be no place for those of his choice.

From the men and women he had known in the past he had to listen not only to congratulations but to a memory or an anecdote of his father or his mother or a tale of his own misdemeanours when he was a small boy.

It all took time and only when the last scullery-boy had had his hand shaken and they had all dispersed towards their various duties in the Abbey did the Butler, who had been a footman in his father's day, say:

"There is champagne in the Dining-Room, M'Lord, and the Chef is ready to cook anything you and Her Ladyship might fancy."

"We have only just finished eating," Lord Vernham said, "but a glass of champagne would, I am sure, be very palatable."

He felt he had not only eaten but also drunk enough at the Wedding Breakfast, for Theobold Muir's wines had been as superlative as his food, but he felt his own staff would be disappointed if he refused all refreshment, so taking Jarita by the arm he led her towards the small Dining-Room.

As he touched her he was aware that she shuddered and made a movement, hastily repressed, to draw away from him.

He felt surprised but he said nothing and when they entered the Dining-Room he wondered if she noticed the lack of furniture.

There were however on the table two lighted candelabra which he recognized as being from the Verne collection.

They held six candles each and he looked at them in

delight, knowing he had never expected to see them again.

Almost automatically he took the glass of champagne that was offered him, then raised it towards Jarita, who was standing at his side.

"Welcome to the Abbey!" he said quietly. "I hope you will be very happy here."

"Th-thank . . . you."

He could hardly hear the response, then she took a tiny sip of the champagne and set the glass down on the table.

Lord Vernham thought, although he might have been mistaken, that she swayed a little as she did so.

"I expect you are tired," he said sympathetically. "It may seem early to retire, but I feel sure you would like to do so. We have both had a very long day."

He thought as he spoke he would tell her later about his animals, but at his suggestion Jarita moved immediately towards the door.

The Butler opened it for her and as she walked across the Hall Lord Vernham asked:

"Is there someone to show Her Ladyship to her bed-room?"

"Mrs. Williams is at the top of the stairs, M'Lord."

"Then she will certainly be all right," Lord Vernham said.

Mrs. Williams had looked after his mother and he had been delighted the previous day to find that she was still living in the village and extremely bored, she told him, at having to retire at the age of sixty.

"Let me come back, M'Lord," she pleaded. "I've known the Abbey since I was a child. I went to work there when I was twelve."

"There is nothing I would like better, Mrs. Williams," Lord Vernham had answered, "and I want to re-engage everyone, if possible, who has had anything to do with the house and the Estate in the past."

"That won't be hard, M'Lord, 'though most of the

trained girls are married by now with children of their own. But I'll soon get the younger ones into shape, if Your Lordship will leave it to me."

"That is exactly what I wish to do, Mrs. Williams," Lord Vernham replied.

Now he thought that Mrs. Williams was just the person he should have chosen to look after his wife and perhaps help her not to feel so shy. He had not expected any daughter of Theobold Muir to be so quiet or so subdued.

Now that he was alone he walked to the window to look out, thinking that he was glad the day was over although he had the feeling that new problems were just about to begin.

The setting sun was very beautiful behind the trees in the Park and he decided that he would go out and look at his animals to be quite certain they were comfortable, and not upset by their new surroundings.

He turned towards the door and as he did so his eye alighted on something glittering on the floor.

He picked it up and found it was a large diamond, and a very valuable one.

It must have fallen from Jarita's tiara, he thought, or perhaps from the other jewellery which she wore at her wrist and on her breast.

He had not noticed them particularly, but he thought that every time she moved she glittered, which was appropriate seeing how rich she was.

When she undressed she might miss the diamond and he worried about it, and he decided it would be kind, if nothing else, to set her mind at rest before he went outside.

He crossed the Hall and climbing the stairs walked down the long, empty corridor which led from the centre of the Abbey towards the South Wing.

It was quite a distance to walk and Lord Vernham thought, as he did so, how different the house would soon look with the pictures and furniture restored and new carpets on the floors, which at the moment all needed polishing.

There was a door which shut off the South Wing completely from the other part of the house and he opened it to find a smally lobby off which opened two doors—one which led into his own bed-room, the other to Jarita's.

He knocked on the latter and almost immediately the door was opened by Mrs. Williams.

"Your Lordship!" She smiled and curtseyed.

"Good-evening, Mrs. Williams. I have brought Her Ladyship something which must have fallen out of her tiara or a bracelet. I thought she might be worried about it."

He opened his hand as he spoke so that Mrs. Williams could see the large diamond glittering in his palm.

"A diamond, M'Lord!"

"Exactly!" Lord Vernham replied.

"I'll give it to Her Ladyship when she comes back upstairs," Mrs. Williams said, taking it from him, "but I thought she was with Your Lordship."

"With me?" Lord Vernham enquired in surprise.

"Yes, M'Lord."

"But I understood you met her on the stairs."

"Yes, M'Lord, I brought her here and Her Ladyship took off her tiara and veil and gave them to me. Then without giving any explanation she left the room. I thought she had gone downstairs again . . . I thought too, M'Lord. . ."

Mrs. Williams paused.

"What did you think?" Lord Vernham enquired.

"Of course I may have been mistaken, but I was a-looking out the window, M'Lord, and I thinks that I sees something white going across the lawn towards the lake. I had the idea Your Lordship were a-taking Her Ladyship for a walk."

For a moment Lord Vernham was still, then he said:

"I will find Her Ladyship, Mrs. Williams, but go to bed. Do not wait up for us."

"You're quite certain, M'Lord?"

"Quite certain, Mrs. Williams!"

Lord Vernham turned away, walked across the lobby, and shut the door behind him.

He hurried down the long passage and when he reached the staircase he began to run.

# Chapter Four

Lord Vernham reached the lake without seeing any sign of Jarita.

It should have been easy even in the fallen darkness to see her white gown and he now thought perhaps Mrs. Williams had been mistaken and she must be somewhere in the house.

Then at the far end of the lake, right out in the centre of the water, he saw something white.

He ran quickly along the path, which was overgrown and difficult to follow. Suddenly he saw a boat; in it Jarita was crouched down and he thought her hands must be over her face.

It was then he realised exactly what she was doing.

The boat was drifting, moving slowly but relentlessly towards the cascade at the end of the lake which fell from there into a whirlpool.

It took just a moment for him to pull off the elegant tight-fitting coat he had worn at his wedding before he plunged into the water, swimming strongly with the swiftness of a man who is in the peak of condition.

He reached the boat as it was gathering speed and turning on the current, and as he put his hands out to hold on to it the sound of his approach must have alerted Jarita.

She stood up to stare at him wildly.

He was just about to speak to her and warn her that she was in danger when with a shrill cry she threw herself out of the boat and into the water on the other side of it.

It took Lord Vernham a few seconds to swim round the boat. He found her thrashing about in the water and realised that she could not swim.

Even as he reached her and she clutched out convulsively to hold on to him, he could feel the strong pull of the current above the cascade and knew that now they were both in danger.

There was nothing he could do but hold Jarita's head down in the water until she no longer struggled and at the same time swim towards the bank.

It was not easy and the effort of pulling Jarita with him and struggling against the suction of the cascade required every ounce of his strength.

For one moment he thought he must fail and they would both be swept down the rushing water and into the whirlpool.

Then with what was an almost superhuman effort he reached the bank and held on to it with his left hand while his right supported the now-still body of Jarita.

He was gasping when finally he dragged her out of the water and onto the grass.

He turned her face downwards and as soon as he got his own breath he started to pump her ribs rhythmically.

It was a method he had been taught by a sea-captain after they had rounded Cape Horn in a tempest, losing two men overboard and saving a third from drowning by this method.

He worked on and after a little time she began to splutter and murmur and he knew she was alive.

He kept on working at her for a little while longer,

then sat back to sweep his wet hair from his forehead and pull his sodden cravat from his neck.

He had lost both his shoes when he had dived into the lake, but he was not concerned about himself but with the prostrate and soaked body of his wife.

She was still lying face downwards and now he stood up to put his hands under her arms and pull her to her feet.

"The sooner you get into dry clothes the better," he said as he did so.

As he spoke she turned her head as if to look at him, then made a little sound that was half a groan, half a cry, and collapsed.

He realised she had fainted and picking her up in his arms he started to walk towards the Abbey.

As he did so he saw the lights which had been glowing golden in all the windows gradually go out one by one and he knew that the workmen must have finished for the day.

It was a good thing, he thought.

There would be no-one about and he had no desire to cause needless comment if it was known what had happened.

He was well aware that the fact that the new Lady Vernham had tried to commit suicide on her wedding-night would be a tit-bit of gossip which would run like wildfire through the village to be repeated and re-repeated round the whole County.

He thought that when he told Mrs. Williams not to wait up for him some instinct must have warned him what might be happening, and now carrying Jarita he knew he had been very obtuse.

He should have realised before that what he had imagined was her shyness was in fact fear.

More than anyone else, because he was used to being with wild animals he should have been able to recognise the signs.

The coldness of her hands, the way her fingers had

trembled in his, the shudder she had given when he touched her, and the manner in which she had winced away from him should have made clear even to a less-experienced man what she was feeling.

Jarita was very light and it did not take him long to reach the house.

She did not stir and he thought if she was still unconscious perhaps it was a good thing.

He remembered the broken latch in the room where he had sat with his uncle and put Jarita down on the long grass of what had once been a lawn to pull open the casement.

He entered the room and from there unlocked one of the long windows in the adjacent Salon.

He knew that by this time of night the only servants he was likely to encounter would be the night-watchmen or a footman on duty in the Hall.

By ascending the secondary staircase he reached the South Wing without being seen.

With Jarita still in his arms he managed to open first the outer door, then the door of her bed-room.

Mrs. Williams had left candles alight beside the bed and the room was bathed in a soft golden light which hid the inadequacy of its furnishings and the threadbare condition of the curtains.

Lord Vernham put Jarita down on the hearth-rug, then collecting some soft towels looked down at her in the light from the candles.

Her face was as white as her gown had been, and her hair, which was longer than he had expected, was falling over her shoulders wet and lank.

What had been a beautiful and expensive gown was now little more than a crumpled rag, marked from the weeds in the lake and the grasses on which she had lain.

Her eyes were firmly closed and he could not determine whether she was still in a faint or in a self-induced coma from a desire not to face reality again.

Either way, he told himself, he must get her out of
her wet clothes unless he wished her to contract pneu-
monia.

He began to rub her hair gently with a towel and as
he did so realised he was making her wetter than necessary from the water dripping from his shirt.

He pulled it off impatiently and naked to the waist
continued to dry Jarita's face and hair before he turned
her over to undo her gown.

He thought with a faint smile as he undid the buttons that he had undressed many women in his life at
one time or another, but never one who was soaked to
the skin and also unconscious.

The buttons were not hard to unfasten and as he
pulled the gown from Jarita's shoulders he was suddenly still from sheer astonishment.

For a moment he thought what he saw must be a
trick of the light, then as he moved to make sure he was
not being deceived he saw the weals on her back and
drew in his breath.

Never in his life had he seen a woman who had been
so brutally mangled.

The weals crossed and recrossed one another, many
of them now bleeding from where they had stuck to
her gown. Others had scabs on them, so he knew that
the cruel treatment she had received must have taken
place a few days ago.

She was marked, he discovered, from her shoulders
to her knees, and he realised that to touch her in any
way even with the softness of a towel might make the
wounds worse.

Instead he spread two dry towels on the bed, then
very carefully lifted her onto them and covered her
completely with another towel before he drew the
sheets and blankets over her.

Only when his task was completed did he stand at
the bed-side to look down at her, still finding it almost

impossible to believe what he had seen with his own eyes.

* * *

Jarita gave a little cry of fear and a voice said quietly:

"It is all right. You are quite safe."

She opened her eyes, saw in the candlelight who was sitting facing her on the bed, and made an incoherent sound in her throat.

At the same time, she pressed herself backwards and the pain of it made her cry out again.

"There is no need to be frightened," Lord Vernham said, "but I would like you to drink this."

He put his hand behind her head as he spoke and held a glass to her lips.

The mere fact that he was touching her made her tremble so much that her teeth chattered against the rim of it, but he tipped it slightly and she felt the liquid flow into her mouth and there was nothing she could do but swallow it.

The brandy seemed to seep through her and although she hated the taste of it she felt as if the darkness which had encompassed her began to recede. Now she not only knew where she was but who was with her.

"Drink it all," Lord Vernham said, and because Jarita was used to obeying orders she did as she was told.

Only when the wine-glass was empty did he set her back against the pillows.

He then sat on the mattress facing her and she stared at him, feeling her heart was beating so loudly that he must hear it.

Looking at her, Lord Vernham thought he had never before seen a woman whose eyes expressed fear so vividly.

They were in fact extraordinary eyes and seemed to fill the whole of her small white face.

She looked quite different from what he had expected: now that her hair had dried the candlelight picked up glints of red in the fairness of it, and he realised that in contrast her long eye-lashes were dark.

However, for the moment he was not concerned with his wife's appearance but the fact that she was obviously so terror-stricken as to be incapable of speech.

She also trembled, and he could see that it was not because she was cold.

He had lit the fire in the grate and the room was very warm, but Jarita's hands as she moved them under the blankets towards her breasts felt bitterly cold.

As she touched her body she realised she was naked.

Her eyes seemed to open even wider, and in a voice which was difficult to hear she asked:

"H-how did you . . . get me . . . here?"

"I saved you from being swept into the whirlpool," Lord Vernham replied in a calm voice. "You may not be aware of it, but there is at the end of the lake a very dangerous whirlpool where several people have been drowned."

He was speaking to reassure her but her eyes flickered and he realised that in fact she had known the whirlpool was dangerous.

"You are far too young to die," he said. "Besides, there is nothing *now* for you to fear."

He accentuated the word "now," hoping she would understand, and after a moment he asked:

"Why did your father beat you?"

He thought she would not answer him. Then almost as if the words were dragged from between her lips she said:

"Y-you will be angry . . . angry if I . . . tell you."

Lord Vernham smiled at her.

"Let me promise you that I will not be angry with you now or at any time."

"You were . . . angry when . . . you were being . . . married to me."

He was surprised that she should have been so perceptive of his feelings

Then he told himself there was something very sensitive about her appearance, and now that he could see her properly there was nothing in the slightest to remind him of her father.

"If I was angry this afternoon let me assure you that it was not with you. I will not be angry now, whatever you tell me."

She looked away from him, then after a moment she said:

"I . . . I did not wish to . . . marry you."

"That I can understand," Lord Vernham answered, "and I assure you, Jarita, it was not my fault that we had no chance to become acquainted before we were actually joined together as man and wife."

"Papa . . . would not . . . allow it?"

He shook his head.

"No."

"Why . . . did you not . . . let me die?"

"Because you are young and life is a very precious thing. There are many amusing and exciting adventures for you in the years ahead. What a pity to waste them."

"I . . . I am . . . your wife."

"Is that so horrifying?"

He saw an expression on her face that he could only translate to himself as one of terror.

"What have they been saying to you? What have you been told about me?" he asked.

She did not reply and after a moment he said:

"Can it be that you are confusing me in your mind with my cousin Gervaise, to whom you were engaged?"

He knew as he spoke that this was indeed the explanation, and the expression on Jarita's face told him far more than words would have done.

"My cousin," he said, choosing his words with care,

"was someone I never liked and of whose actions I invariably disapproved. I may have many faults, Jarita, which I am sure you will discover in time, but I am in fact a very different person from Gervaise."

He tried to speak convincingly, but the terror and horror were still there and after a moment he asked almost sharply:

"What did Gervaise do to you?"

"Not . . . to me," she murmured, "but to B-Betsy . . . and . . . little Mary."

She realised the names meant nothing to him, and after a moment she said, still in that low, almost inaudible voice:

"B-Betsy drowned herself in the . . . whirlpool."

"And little Mary?"

Although he had no desire to ask questions that concerned Gervaise, Lord Vernham knew he must get to the bottom of what was terrifying Jarita.

"M-Mary was only . . . eleven . . . she . . . went mad!"

The words were spoken, then Jarita gave another of her little cries of fear.

"You are . . . angry . . . I knew you would be . . . angry!"

"I am not angry with you," Lord Vernham said quickly, "but with my cousin for the wretched crimes he committed, and the fact that they were recounted to you."

"Papa . . . did not know I had . . . heard about them," Jarita explained, "b-but I knew I could never m-marry him . . . but it is . . . difficult to know how to . . . kill one's self."

"Is that why your father beat you?"

"N-no . . . I ran . . . away," she explained. "I thought I would . . . hide somewhere . . . b-but he rode after me . . . he was determined . . . he has always been . . . determined that I should be L-Lady Vernham."

"And now that you are, there is nothing to be afraid of—least of all of me!"

Her eyes were on his face and he thought that some of the fear was passing from them.

Yet she was watching him warily almost as if she were a wild animal he was trying to tame, alert in case his overtures of friendship were a trap.

"We have both had a long day," Lord Vernham said. "I was very busy this morning with something that I want to show you tomorrow, and you must have found the wedding very tiring."

He paused before he said:

"If I leave you alone to go to sleep, will you give me your word of honor that you will not try to run away and that I can trust you to be here in the morning?"

"Y-you are . . . going to . . . sleep in your . . . own room?"

This, Lord Vernham realised, was the vital question and one she felt compelled to ask even though she was terrified of what his answer might be.

"I am sleeping next door," he replied. "There is a door between our two rooms. If you are frightened of anything in the night or if you feel ill you have only to shout and I will come to you at once. Otherwise I think we both wish to be alone."

She seemed to ponder over this for a moment and then said:

"Did you not . . . wish to . . . marry me?"

"I had no wish to marry anybody," Lord Vernham replied frankly, "and certainly not someone I was not allowed to talk to until my ring was actually on her finger."

"Papa . . . made you . . . marry me."

"Have you no idea of the reason?" Lord Vernham enquired.

Jarita paused for a moment, then she said:

"Was it because you . . . wanted back the things that were in Aladdin's Cave?"

She saw the surprise on his face and explained:

"I mean all the things which . . . had belonged to the Abbey and which Papa kept in a special store at home. I think . . . although nobody ever told me . . . that your uncle sold them to him."

"My uncle not only sold everything that was valuable in this house," Lord Vernham replied, "he also borrowed a great deal of money from your father, as did my cousin Gervaise."

"So you have no . . . money now that you are . . . Lord Vernham?"

"That is the whole story in a nut-shell."

"Now I begin to . . . understand," she said. "I have thought about it for a long time and I guessed that was the . . . explanation, but nobody told me what was . . . happening or why I had to . . . marry you."

She blushed and added quickly:

"I knew of course what . . . Papa wanted for me."

"I think the best thing for both of us is to try to forget the circumstances which forced us into the position in which we find ourselves. Instead, shall we try to enjoy being married?"

"B-but you . . . did not . . . want me as your . . . wife."

"And you certainly did not want me as your husband."

"No . . . that is true . . ."

"At the same time, I do not intend to drown myself in the whirlpool or throw myself from the top of the Abbey," Lord Vernham said. "I have far more interesting plans for the future. Besides, even if you did not miss me, Bella, Ajax, Scobi, and Meena certainly would."

"Who are . . . they?"

Again he smiled.

"Two of them are very attractive ladies," he answered, "but you need not be afraid that they constitute any competition. Meena is a cheetah and Bella is a lioness."

Now Jarita's eyes were round with surprise.

"You mean . . . they are here . . . at the Abbey?"

"They are in the Park, and the reason why I was so busy this morning was that they arrived only a few hours before I was due at the Church. I brought them with me when I returned from Africa."

"They are not . . . dangerous?"

"Not in the slightest! I have brought them up since they were cubs. Tomorrow I will introduce them to you and you will understand how I look on them as my family and how important they are to me."

"I saw lions and tigers once in the Tower of London," Jarita said. "They were in small cages, and they did not seem to be very happy."

"My lions are running loose in large enclosures in the Park," Lord Vernham said. "It will not be the same as having an enormous jungle to themselves, but I think they will be happy because they are with me."

"It is very . . . strange that you should have lions and cheetahs as . . . pets."

"A great many people have kept them as pets before me," Lord Vernham smiled, "but I will tell you all about that tomorrow. Now, Jarita, I want you to go to sleep. You promise that you will still be here in the morning?"

"Yes . . . I promise."

The answer came quickly and he knew it was genuine.

"As I have already told you, there are many unusual and exciting things for us to do together. At the same time, we shall get to know each other."

Lord Vernham's eyes were on hers as he said:

"I hope very much, Jarita, that although we have started our marriage on what some people would call the 'wrong foot,' we will be able to become friends."

"Do you . . . mean that? I have . . . never had a friend . . . at least I do not think so."

"I mean it in all sincerity," he replied, "and as a friend can you think of a good explanation we can give for your wedding-gown being that wet rag I see lying on the hearth-rug?"

Jarita raised herself a little on the pillows to look at it and winced as she did so. Lord Vernham knew it was because her back was so painful.

He thought, however, that it was best not to refer to it again, and after a moment she said:

"C-could . . . we say that in the dark I fell into the lake . . . by mistake . . . and that you rescued me?"

"I think that seems a perfectly reasonable explanation, and one which Mrs. Williams will accept since she saw you in the garden."

"Perhaps I could say that I was looking for . . . you in the Park where you had gone to see the lions?"

"That makes the story even better," Lord Vernham approved. "If you can make it sound convincing there will be no gossip about what has happened, which I think we should both appreciate."

"I forgot that what I did would cause . . . scandal for you," Jarita said. "I . . . I am sorry."

"Fortunately it is something we shall be able to avoid," Lord Vernham replied. "Now I am going to cope with my own wet things. I am afraid my wedding-garments are irretrievably ruined."

She would have apologised again but saw that his eyes were twinkling and he was smiling.

"It is not a disaster," he added, "because I have no intention of getting married again. Once is quite enough!"

With an effort Jarita managed a very faint smile.

He rose from the bed, moving slowly in case he should frighten her.

"Good night, Jarita," he said in his deep voice, "and

do not forget, if you want anything you have only to call me."

He walked to the fireplace to put another log on the fire and knew that she was watching him. Then he turned and opened the communicating door between their two rooms.

"Sleep well," he said, and left her alone.

Jarita lay for a long time listening to him moving about next door. Then finally he must have blown out the light, for his room was in darkness and she turned to extinguish the candles by her own bed-side.

As she sat up she was conscious that her back hurt intolerably with every moment she made and realised once again that she was naked.

She felt herself blushing at the thought of who had undressed her! It was almost impossible to believe that it was a man who had taken off her clothes and seen the whip-marks on her back.

It was something so shameful and so immodest that her first impulse was to hide herself away and never see Lord Vernham again.

Then she told herself sensibly that she had in fact meant nothing to him as a woman.

Why should he, when he had hated the idea of marrying her as much as she had hated the idea of marrying him?

In her terror at having to do what her father had ordered, she had, until he had spoken to her just now, never considered his feelings.

The stories she had heard about Gervaise had made her suppose that all noblemen were the same, ready to force themselves on any girl or woman who took their fancy, regardless of her class or circumstances.

As was to be expected, Jarita was very innocent and and all she knew about the passions or interests of men was what she had learnt from Emma.

But the books she had read had told her there must be something men and women did together to produce

children, and she had assumed it was something very
intimate and private that, with a man like Gervaise
Verne, would be terrifying.

But Lord Vernham was different . . . very different,
and he had said he wanted them to be friends.

'That is what I would like him to be,' she thought.

Although she had extinguished the candles, there was
still the firelight and she was glad that she was not completely in the dark.

"I need no longer be afraid," she told herself, "and
if I am, I have only to call out and he will come to me."

She thought about this for some time, then she decided it would be very stupid to go on being frightened
of him.

He was, it was true, very large, but she had studied
his face and knew there was something about him
which told her she could trust him.

"I am his wife . . . I am . . . married," she whispered.

She felt again that little quiver of fear that the word
"marriage" had evoked when her father had spoken
of it.

But here in the firelight nothing was as fearful as
she had anticipated.

'Tomorrow he will show me his lions,' she thought,
and fell asleep thinking of them.

*        *        *

"Just stand quite still beside me," Lord Vernham
said. "Do not make a hasty movement until they have
learnt to accept you."

He had opened the door into the lions' enclosure and
although Jarita felt as if there were butterflies fluttering inside her she walked in bravely, determined that
Lord Vernham should not realise she was in fact very
frightened.

The moment they appeared, Ajax came bounding
from the far end of the enclosure.

"He will not hurt you," Lord Vernham said, and it was obvious that Ajax was not interested in anybody but his master.

He stood up on his hind-legs and put his paws on Lord Vernham's shoulders, who patted him affectionately, running his fingers through his mane before he said:

"Sit, Ajax!"

The lion obeyed him. Then he said to Jarita:

"Put out your hand."

She obeyed him although she could not help a little tremor as she did so.

"This is a friend, Ajax," Lord Vernham said, "and a very important friend to us both."

As if he understood what he said, the lion looked at Jarita, then licked her hand. His tongue felt very rough on her soft skin.

"Now you are introduced," Lord Vernham said, "and you can pat him as you would your dog."

"I have never had a dog."

Lord Vernham raised his eye-brows.

"Why not?"

"Papa thought it would distract me from my lessons, and they were very important."

"Why?"

She glanced at him from under her eye-lashes.

"I was being highly educated . . . to be . . . a Lady of . . . Title."

"And now you are one?"

"I find I am lamentably ignorant about lions," she replied with a flash of humour he had not expected.

"That is something which must obviously be remedied. I am afraid you cannot yet meet Bella, because she has cubs. They were born during the voyage and she hides them even from me."

He looked towards a clump of shrubs at the far end of the enclosure and almost as if he had called her a very beautiful lioness emerged from among the leaves.

"Are you not coming to talk to me, Bella?" Lord Vernham enquired.

The lioness walked slowly towards him. Then she rubbed herself against his legs with a gesture that was extremely affectionate.

Jarita looked at Ajax a little nervously and because she did not wish to be a coward she forced herself to put out her hand towards his mane.

He accepted her touch for a few minutes, then bounded towards his master.

The cheetahs with their spotted coats and curved tails were full of tricks which Lord Vernham had taught them. They climbed up one of the trees at his command and jumped with a grace that was indescribable onto the top of their flat-topped house.

Meena seemed to twine herself round him and they both accepted Jarita in a manner which swept away her fear of them.

She saw that their enclosure had a higher fence and was constructed so that they could not scramble or leap over it.

"When they grow more accustomed to their surroundings," Lord Vernham said, "we will take them into the house. But I think for the moment they would frighten the workmen, even if they were on a lead."

"I am sure the men would be terrified of them," Jarita agreed. "Do you often let them loose?"

"In Africa they went everywhere with me," Lord Vernham replied, "but here if they were free they would attack the deer. It is in their nature to hunt. It is what they have been bred for, and I think they find it very unsporting that they do not have to get their meal by first killing it."

"They are very beautiful!" Jarita remarked.

"To the ancient Egyptians they exemplified courage," Lord Vernham explained. "While the lion was the emblem of Royalty and authority, there are only two records of a cheetah becoming a Royal pet."

"Who, then, did show such good taste?" Jarita asked.

"Genghis Khan and the Emperor Charlemagne."

"You are certainly in distinguished company!" she smiled.

The cheetahs rolled on their back so that Jarita and Lord Vernham could scratch their chests.

While they did so, their whole bodies vibrated, and breathing in and out they gave what Lord Vernham said was the famous cheetah purr.

Meena finally nibbled his ear, which he told Jarita was a sign of great affection.

When they said good-bye Jarita thought the cheetahs looked reproachful because they must be locked in and could not accompany their master as they expected to do.

There was still the parrot-house in the Orangery to see and Jarita went into ecstasies over the dazzling plumage of the birds.

There was one large macaw which flew immediately as they entered to sit on Lord Vernham's shoulder.

"He is very beautiful!" Jarita said admiringly as she looked at his blue and red tail.

"You're a fool!" the parrot said rudely, and Jarita laughed.

"So he talks!"

"Quite a lot of them do when they are alone with me," Lord Vernham replied. "This old rascal, whose name is Horatio, is ready to swear at anyone if it suits him, and I am afraid he is not very polite."

He brought Horatio in from the Orangery and put him on a perch in the Hall.

"He will be much happier here. He likes to have people round him. It will amuse him to swear at the footmen, and he will soon learn how to call one in my voice or in the Butler's, and the wretched young man will not know who is giving orders!"

"I would like to hear him do that now," Jarita said excitedly.

"You will have to wait until he has perfected his repertoire in English," Lord Vernham said. "The servants he called in Africa were black boys, and they used to get furious with him!"

Lord Vernham noticed as they went into luncheon that Jarita was more animated and certainly happier than he had seen her look before.

The day that followed their wedding he had made her stay in bed and as she had slept most of the time he was aware it was a wise decision.

Mrs. Williams and everybody else had accepted the story that in looking for her husband, who she had thought was with the lions, she had in the dark fallen into the lake.

"It was so stupid of me," Jarita said.

"It must have been a shock, M'Lady," Mrs. Williams replied, "and on top of the wedding it might have been a real upset to your system."

Although there were many things Jarita wanted to see, she had in fact the following day felt very limp and although she did not complain her back was very painful.

She knew too that she was suffering a reaction from the fear and terror that had possessed her ever since she had known that she was to be married.

It was a thought that had menaced her by day and by night, and even before her father beat her she had slept very little.

After that, lying on her face because it was agony to touch her back, it had been impossible.

Miss Dawson had applied every sort of salve and lotion, but there was nothing they could do to prevent the way in which the scars stiffened or the fact that as they began to heal they itched.

What added to Jarita's unhappiness was the fact that her father had vented his wrath not only on her but also on Miss Dawson.

"What are you going to do when I am married, Dawsie?" she asked.

"I am to leave immediately after the wedding-ceremony," Miss Dawson replied.

"Has Papa told you to do that?"

"He would have sent me away before, but you were so ill after he punished you that I think he was frightened you would not be on your feet for the day of the wedding."

"He has dismissed you?" Jarita asked in horror.

Somehow, despite what Miss Dawson had said, she had believed her father would keep her at Kingsclere just in case she was wanted.

"He has not only dismissed me," Miss Dawson replied, "but has forfeited my wages for this month and refuses to give me a reference."

She gave a little sigh.

"You know what that means, dearest. It will be very difficult for me to get other employment."

"How could Papa do anything so unkind?" Jarita cried.

It was a foolish question; she knew her father would always do what he wished to do, and was, if opposed, very vindictive.

Suddenly there was a light in her eyes.

"You need not worry about a reference, darling Dawsie," she exclaimed. "I can give you one!"

Miss Dawson gave a little laugh and sat down in an adjacent chair.

"So you can. I never thought of that."

They looked at each other and they were both thinking that in this way, if in no other, they could score over Mr. Muir.

"As soon as I am married I will write you the most wonderful reference anybody ever had," Jarita promised.

She was thinking of this conversation as luncheon finished, and as they rose from the table she said in the nervous tone which Lord Vernham was beginning to recognise:

"I . . . I have something to . . . ask you."

He waited.

"You may . . . refuse," she said, "but if it is possible . . . could I give a little money to my old Governess . . . only a little?"

Her eyes were raised beseechingly to his face as she continued:

`"Because I . . . ran away, Papa dismissed her without a reference . . . and confiscated the money that was owed her for the last month she was with me."

Lord Vernham's lips tightened.

The more he learnt about Theobold Muir, the more he knew that he loathed and despised a man who would beat anybody so sensitive and fragile as Jarita, and who would punish an employee for an action which was no fault of hers.

"You are angry!" Jarita exclaimed with a little cry of dismay. "I . . . I am . . . sorry I asked you. I did not wish . . . to annoy you."

"I want to talk to you, Jarita," Lord Vernham said.

He drew her away from the Dining-Room, where he thought perhaps the servants might overhear their conversation, into the Sitting-Room, where he had talked with his uncle the first day he had returned to the Abbey.

It looked very different now.

The furniture which had been sold had been replaced and had been recovered in a crimson damask.

Above the panelling there were pictures of the Swaynes dating back for many centuries and the antique furniture of walnut or rosewood made each piece a delight to behold.

As Lord Vernham shut the door behind them he was aware that Jarita's large worried eyes saw nothing but the expression on his face.

"Will you sit down," he suggested.

She obeyed him, and he realised as she clasped her hands together in her lap that it was because she wanted to stop them from trembling.

"The first night we were married," he began, "I told you that you need never be afraid of me. I want you to remember that, Jarita, and to know that whatever you say to me, whatever you ask me, I would never be angry with you."

"Y-you . . . looked . . . angry."

"I was angry that your father should have behaved in a manner which quite frankly I consider diabolical. I have not said this to you before, Jarita, but I intend to say it now. I dislike your father and it is impossible for me to refrain from telling you so."

"Then you are not . . . angry because I asked you for . . . money?"

"That is something else I wish you to understand," Lord Vernham replied. "The money I am spending here on the Abbey is yours. I know that legally I have complete control over it because I am your husband, but your father made your marriage a business arrangement, which I think it is important for us to remember."

Jarita looked puzzled and he said:

"I received your money in exchange for my title."

He smiled as he added:

"Personally, I consider it a poor bargain considering how great your fortune is! But your father was satisfied, and therefore, as far as I am concerned, everything that appertains to the Abbey and the Estate is owned by us jointly—half mine and half yours, Jarita."

He had learnt by now that she was intelligent and quick-brained.

As she grasped what he was saying there was a new light in her eyes, and her expression, which had been nervous and fearful, became one of incredulous delight.

"Do you really mean that?" she asked.

"Of course I mean it," he answered, "and I want you always to remember it, especially as regards money."

"Then I may send Dawsie some?"

"As much as you like."

Jarita glanced at him to see if he was serious, then she said hesitatingly:

"Would . . . one hundred pounds be too much?"

"I was actually going to suggest two hundred, considering she has looked after you for so many years," Lord Vernham replied. "Or if you wish, you can work it out for each year she has spent in your service. That is usually done when someone leaves a legacy after they are dead."

"I think Dawsie would be overjoyed to receive two hundred pounds," Jarita replied. "If I offered her more she might refuse to take it."

"If she is the sort of person I imagine her to be, that is quite a possibility," Lord Vernham agreed.

"Can I send it to her now . . . this moment?"

He made a gesture with his hand.

"There is nothing to stop you."

"Oh, you are so kind . . . how can I thank you?"

"You do not have to. As I have just explained—it is your money."

"A lot of men would not behave as you are doing."

He knew that for a brief second she was thinking of Gervaise, and he replied gravely:

"I have already told you I am different—at least I hope so."

That evening as they were finishing dinner Holden came into the room to whisper something in Lord Vernham's ear.

He listened to what his valet had to say and almost immediately rose to his feet.

"Will you excuse me, Jarita?" he asked, and went from the Dining-Room.

She felt a little perplexed by his abrupt departure and she also wished he had asked her to go with him.

What could have happened? Had one of the work-

men asked for his help? Had something gone wrong in
the work they were doing to the house?

There was so much to do and for Lord Vernham to
supervise that the hours of the day had, Jarita thought,
seemed to speed past.

That afternoon they had ridden out to one of the
farms to find that the new roof had already been
erected and the workmen were busy painting the windows and doors.

They were in fact making the house so attractive that
she almost wished they could live in it themselves.

"I would like to be a farmer's wife," she had said as
they rode home again.

"You would have to work very hard," Lord Vernham smiled.

"I am sure that is better than having nothing to do.
You work hard. That is why I think you are so happy."

"That is very perceptive of you," Lord Vernham answered. "I have in fact worked hard in one way or
another all my life. Perhaps the hardest thing I ever had
to do was to climb a mountain in Afghanistan with
some very obstinate yaks that had to be pulled or
pushed most of the way."

He smiled at the memory and went on:

"I also had a number of porters who were afraid of
the ghouls and djinns who they believed were planning
revenge on us from the tops of the mountains."

Jarita had laughed as he had intended her to do.

He felt that every time she laughed the fear which
still sometimes lingered in her eyes receded a little further.

Although she was beginning to trust him, he knew
that when he went rather too near to her or touched
her by mistake she started and all the uncertainty and
apprehension was there as it had been before.

It was not like training a cub, which was naturally
trusting, he told himself. It was more like taking a wild

animal from the jungle and getting it used to the presence of a human being.

Jarita finished luncheon and went into the Sitting-Room. She wondered what was happening—what was keeping Lord Vernham. She felt suddenly lost and anxious without him.

Without intending to she had begun to rely on him to be there and to prevent her from being lonely.

She caught a glimpse of herself in one of the gold-framed mirrors and for the first time wondered if he found her attractive.

It was difficult for her to judge what she looked like to a man.

Her eyes were certainly very large, but that, she knew, was partially because her face was so thin.

It had been impossible to eat when she was so worried and afraid after she had known about Gervaise Verne.

Her skin was very white and clear, and her hair, now that she was so much happier and less nervous, seemed to have brilliant lights in it that had not been there before.

"Perhaps he does not admire fair women," Jarita reflected. "He has been so long abroad either in the East or in Africa and he doubtless prefers dark hair."

The thought was curiously disspiriting. Then while she was still wondering about herself Lord Vernham came in.

He was holding something in his arms. She waited for him to reach her side, her eyes raised to his.

He smiled down at her.

"I have brought you some work to do."

Jarita saw in surprise that he held a lion cub in his arms. It was not much bigger than a kitten, only its head seemed out of proportion to its body.

She put out her hands, then found it in her arms nestling against her as if it needed her protection.

"Holden is preparing a bottle with which you can feed it," Lord Vernham said.

"But Bella . . . ?" Jarita questioned.

"I must explain," he said. "A lioness usually has four cubs, but invariably one dies soon after birth and one is very weak. That is why it is usual to see a lioness accompanied by only two off-spring. This one, as you see, is too small to assert itself and unless we keep it alive it will die."

Jarita was listening intently.

"Dan, whom I have been teaching to look after the lions, noticed that the other cubs had pushed it aside, and it has had nothing to eat all day."

"Poor little baby!" Jarita murmured.

She held the cub, which was whimpering, closer against her. It had its eyes open and looked like a small ball of spotted fur.

"I thought you would want to save it," Lord Vernham said. "It will mean quite a lot of hard work, but that, I think, is something you have been asking for."

It was certainly enjoyable work, Jarita thought later, as the cub sucked empty the bottle of warm milk that Holden brought her, then fell asleep.

"Will you have it with you tonight?" Lord Vernham asked.

"Of course!" Jarita replied.

"If it grows restless," he said, "put your finger in its mouth. It will suck that quite happily while you ring for Holden to bring another bottle. He does not mind being woken up."

"Where are you going?" Jarita asked as he walked towards the door.

"To have a look at Bella," he replied. "I may be mistaken, but even with Ajax at her side, I am conceited enough to believe that sometimes she needs me."

He was joking, but when he had gone it suddenly occurred to Jarita that she needed him too.

# Chapter Five

Lord Vernham looked into the Sitting-Room.

Jarita was on the floor playing with Bobo.

Having been well fed the last few days, he looked very different from the half-starved little cub he had brought in from the lions' enclosure.

Jarita turned round with a smile and said:

"We are having an expensive morning. Bobo had eaten one of my gloves, torn two pairs of slippers to pieces, and has made a hole in the bed-spread. Mrs. Williams is very angry."

Lord Vernham laughed.

"You will have to give him stronger toys."

"They would need to be made of granite."

"I am just taking a farmer I have interviewed to Elm Tree Farm," Lord Vernham said. "When I come back we will exercise the cheetahs."

Jarita's face lit up.

"I would like to do that. The chains arrived this morning. They are very light and are, I think, just what you required.'

"Good!" Lord Vernham replied. "I will not be long."

He shut the door and Jarita picked up the lion cub and held him against her face. He smelt of honey and

98

already she loved him as she had not thought she could love an animal.

She had never had a pet of her own and the fact that Bobo depended on her had made her feel there was something very special in possessing one.

At the same time, she had grown very fond of the cheetahs.

Lord Vernham had worried about their not having enough exercise and he thought it might be an idea to take them out on a long lead when he and Jarita went riding.

It was impossible for them to run free as he would have wished, because of the deer.

Also there was always the chance that however well trained, they might go too far and frighten some of the men working in the field and the children who were often with them.

He and Jarita had therefore tried leading the cheetahs from the horses on very long ropes. Although they wanted to run faster they were restricted to the rate at which the horses galloped.

The only difficulty was that the moment the horses slowed down or stopped, the cheetahs gnawed through their ropes and escaped.

Lord Vernham had therefore sent for some very thin chains and both he and Jarita were looking forward to trying them out.

"There are so many exciting things to do here," Jarita said to Bobo.

She had grown into the way of talking to him when they were alone.

"It is thrilling," she went on, "to see the rooms altering every day. The Long Gallery is now the most beautiful place I have ever imagined."

Bobo snuggled against her and she said:

"Come along. We must go out in the fresh air. We will see what is happening in the garden."

She carried him into the Hall. Then as she went

towards the front door she saw on the table a large bowl of carrots and apples.

They had been put there on Lord Vernham's instructions so that if either of them wished to go to the stables they could have something to give to the horses.

"We will go to the stables first, Bobo," Jarita said. "I want to see Kingfisher."

This was a new horse which Lord Vernham had bought two days earlier and which he intended for special use.

He was a magnificent roan with a long tail and flowing mane, and Jarita was thrilled with him, especially as he had been trained for a lady's use and was very gentle and easy to handle.

She picked up several carrots and carrying Bobo under her arm walked out into the sunshine.

It was not a long distance to the stables and when she reached the yard she found the horses that were not on exercise looking out over the half-doors of their stalls.

There were no stable-lads about, for this was the time in the morning when they exercised the horses in the Park.

Jarita put Bobo down on the ground and patted Kingfisher with one hand, handing him a carrot with the other.

He seemed to know her already and it was exciting to think he was to be her special mount and that Lord Vernham had personally chosen him for her.

"There are a lot of horses I want to buy," he had said, "but it is important that I should purchase yours first."

"You are spoiling me!" she protested.

"I think it would be impossible to do that," he replied. "I have a feeling that you have not been spoiled nearly enough in the past, and I have to make up for a lot of lost time."

It was the sort of thing he said which thrilled her because no-one had ever talked to her like that.

Her father had ordered her about and he had always made her feel that his concern for her was due only to his ambition for her to make a splendid marriage and was not anything personal.

She was clever enough to realize that Lord Vernham was deliberately making her a partner in everything he undertook.

At the end of each day when they inspected the work that had been done in the Abbey he asked her opinion and deferred to her judgement.

It was something which had never happened to her before and at first she felt too shy to say what she thought.

Then when she realised he genuinely wanted to hear her ideas and her opinions, she gave them, watching him warily in case she should say anything which displeased him.

But she felt a warm sense of satisfaction when she knew the suggestions she made met with his approval.

On the Estate too, he kept her informed of every development.

The only thing he did alone was to interview the farmers who were applying to be tenants on the newly renovated farms.

"When they bring their wives I would like you to meet them," Lord Vernham said, "but otherwise it is easier for me to talk to them man-to-man."

"Yes, of course," Jarita agreed. "And I must admit that the cultivation of the crops is another blank spot in my education."

"There are really quite a number of them," Lord Vernham teased.

She made a little grimace at him.

"If you only knew the hours and hours I have spent poring over books, listening to prosy teachers, and struggling with my homework after they left, you would understand it is very frustrating to feel there are any gaps in my knowledge."

"Thank goodness for them," he replied. "I am frightened of clever women."

"If I am clever it is in the unpractical things, while you . . ."

She made a little gesture with her hand.

"What about me?" he asked curiously.

"You know so much about everything that is important," she murmured. "About people—I have met so few—about wild animals, and of course about running an Estate and making the Abbey the most beautiful place in the world."

"You really feel that?" he asked in a deep voice.

"I have never been so happy."

Then she saw the question in his eyes and blushed.

"How could I have known, how could I have guessed," she asked, "that you would be so . . . different from what I . . . feared?"

She spoke with an intense note in her voice but he answered her lightly.

"Let that teach you yet another lesson, not to judge anyone too hastily," he said. "If you had read your fairy-stories more carefully you would have known that the Beast always turns out to be Prince Charming in disguise."

He laughed, but later that night when she was alone Jarita had told herself he was right. She had thought he would be a beast like his cousin, Gervaise Verne.

Instead he had turned out to be everything that was kind and considerate, and every day she became less and less afraid of him.

She patted Kingfisher's neck as he nuzzled her for more carrots.

"You are greedy!' she said to him. "You will have to wait until after you have had a lot of exercise this afternoon before I give you anything more."

She patted him again and looked for Bobo to pick him up, but he was no longer there.

Instead she saw him on the other side of the stables between two buildings.

"Bobo!" she called, and ran after him.

He hurried away from her, knowing quite well he was doing something naughty.

On the other side of the stable there was a lot of rough grass and weeds which would later have to be cleared away when the gardeners had time to spare from the enormous amount there was to be done nearer the house.

With an instinct to hide which was born in him, Bobo moved into the long grass.

Jarita had almost reached him and could see him moving through the weeds and nettles, when suddenly there was a loud crack and Bobo gave a cry of fear and disappeared.

Jarita had only to go a few more steps to see what had happened.

Amongst the debris there was a circular wooden cover which was broken and had a hole in the middle of it.

It was through this that Bobo had disappeared.

She knelt down, and pulling the wood, which came apart in her hands, she saw that it covered a large hole.

Throwing the wood to one side, she saw that it was a well.

It was obviously disused and like everything else at the Abbey its cover had deteriorated and had not been repaired or replaced.

She bent over the well, her voice frightened as she called:

"Bobo! Bobo!"

In response she heard the cub growling and whining. The fall had not killed him, and what was even more merciful, there was obviously little or no water in the well.

She looked round, intending to call for help, when she saw there was a ladder fixed to one side of the brick interior.

"It is all right, Bobo," she cried. "I will come down and fetch you. Do not be frightened."

Jarita was not afraid of climbing ladders or for that matter of heights.

In fact Miss Dawson had often rebuked her for running along the top of the high walls which enclosed the kitchen-garden at Kingsclere and for climbing up to the roof of the house to look at the view.

She had never climbed down into a well before but she imagined because she could hear Bobo quite clearly that it was not very deep.

Once she had her feet on the rungs of the ladder she began to descend rapidly.

Then when she was halfway down she heard an ominous crack. She tightened her hold as the ladder broke at the top and swung away from the side.

She gave a scream of fear as she hung suspended across the darkness of the well. Then she felt herself falling and knew no more. . . .

* * *

Lord Vernham returned to the Abbey well satisfied with the new tenant-farmer he had accepted for Elm Tree Farm.

He was a Scotsman, his references were excellent, and Lord Vernham was certain he was just the right type of man they wanted to put into working order the land that had been neglected for so long.

"You may wish to bring your wife with you to see the house before you finally decide it will suit you," Lord Vernham had suggested.

The Scotsman shook his head.

"My wife'll be verra pleased, M'Lord, as I am both with the house and the prospect of having Your Lordship as our landlord."

It was the sort of compliment Lord Vernham appreciated.

He decided if they could find for the remaining farms six more men as suitable as this one, the Vernham Estate would soon recover the reputation it had enjoyed in his grandfather's time.

He had driven the farmer over to Elm Tree Farm in a Curricle and as he handed the reins to a groom who was waiting for him at the front door he said:

"Bring round Kingfisher and Rufus in a quarter of an hour; Her Ladyship and I will ride before luncheon."

"Very good, M'Lord."

"And send word to Dan that I will take the cheetahs with me."

Lord Vernham walked into the house. As he gave his hat and driving-gloves to a footman he thought with a smile there were few women who would find a quarter of an hour time enough in which to change into their riding-clothes.

But he had learnt that Jarita was very quick, in fact she never kept him waiting.

He thought he would find her in the Sitting-Room, but it was empty and he went back into the Hall to ask a footman:

"Have you seen Her Ladyship?"

"She went out about half an hour ago, M'Lord."

"I expect she is in the garden," Lord Vernham said.

He found what seemed almost an army of gardeners: several were making the lawns look like green velvet as they had in the past, others were cutting away the overgrown shrubs which had encroached until in some places they reminded him of a jungle.

Half a dozen were bedding out plants they had

been forced to buy because it was too late in the year to grow them from seed.

It was amazing what a difference had been accomplished in such a short time, but Lord Vernham was aware there was still a great deal to do.

He remembered his grandmother saying once:

"One can never hurry nature."

That was true, and he thought that it would be next year before the garden would become a worthy setting for the Abbey.

"Have you seen Her Ladyship?" he asked one of the men cutting away at a yew-hedge.

"No, M'Lord, not this mornin'."

"She will be in the stables," Lord Vernham told himself.

He might have guessed, he thought, that Jarita would want to feed her new horse.

He had been very fortunate that someone had told him that that particular horse was for sale privately, and he had felt rewarded for the trouble he had gone to in buying it when saw the excitement in Jarita's eyes.

But he told himself as he walked towards the stables that it was really Bobo who had transformed her.

It had been both luck and inspiration on his part to give her the cub to look after. The terror he had seen in her eyes when they were married had, for the moment, disappeared, and he hoped and prayed it would never return.

He thought that by now, although he did not like to ask, Jarita's back must be better.

Watching her, he noticed that she sat more comfortably and leaned back against a sofa or a chair as she had been unable to do at first.

One great relief was that there had been no sign or word from Theobold Muir.

Lord Vernham imagined that Jarita's father was being tactful as officially they were on their honeymoon, but Lord Vernham had already resolved that he would make it very clear in the future that he was not welcome at the Abbey.

It would be impossible to keep him away altogether, but Lord Vernham was sure that his presence would have an adverse effect on Jarita and that he was determined to prevent at any cost.

Lord Vernham reached the stables and as he did so a number of horses ridden by grooms came in at the far end.

He looked at them without much interest.

They were mostly horses lent to him by his father-in-law, and he was determined to return them as soon as he was able to build up his own stable.

At the same time, horses were needed to draw his Phaeton and Curricle for him, and for Jarita to ride and for the grooms who had innumerable messages to carry.

Besides this, the wagons wanted pulling, as did the Landaus, which were used to bring food to the house and also to transport a great number of materials which were demanded by the workmen every day.

"It is no use cutting off my nose to spite my face," Lord Vernham told himself.

At the same time, he knew he would feel very much happier when the stables were filled with horses that belonged only to Jarita and himself.

The Head-groom, having dismounted, came hurrying towards him.

"Good-mornin', M'Lord. Is there anythin' I can do for Your Lordship?"

"I thought Her Ladyship must be here," Lord Vernham replied. "I have already sent instructions to say that we wish to ride Kingfisher and Rufus immediately."

The Head-groom glanced towards the stables.

"They're being saddled, M'Lord."

"Then perhaps Her Ladyship is with her horse," Lord Vernham remarked.

But there was no sign of Jarita, and when he had looked in almost every stall because he felt certain she must be there somewhere, Lord Vernham returned to the house.

He supposed that Jarita must have gone to see what the workmen were doing, but it was unlike her because she usually waited so that they could go together in the evening.

But no-one had seen any sign of her. He looked into the Long Gallery and the Library, searched the Orangery, and even walked down to the enclosures to see if she was talking to the lions or the cheetahs.

Dan was trying out the long chains on the latter and both cheetahs had collars round their necks.

They bounded towards their master and Lord Vernham said quickly:

"I am not ready for them yet, Dan. I am trying to find Her Ladyship."

"She's not been here this morning, M'Lord."

As he walked back to the house Lord Vernham began to worry.

Could it be possible that Jarita had run away?

He could not credit she would do such a thing, because he was sure that she had spoken the truth when she had said she was happier than she had ever been before in her life.

Then where could she be?

There must be some quite ordinary explanation, he told himself.

He was quite certain that if in fact some wild notion had made her want to escape she would not have taken Bobo with her.

"Something must have happened to them both," he muttered.

It was unlikely that they had got shut into a room by mistake and been unable to get out.

Nearly every door in the Abbey had needed new locks and keys and most of them had not yet been fitted.

He went back to the stables feeling somehow that it was here Jarita had gone, although he had no reason to be sure of anything.

Kingfisher and Rufus were now saddled and waiting in the yard and the grooms and stable-boys were standing in a cluster round them, discussing, Lord Vernham was sure, the mystery of Jarita's disappearance.

As he walked up to them there was a sudden silence and several of them moved away as if afraid he might enquire why they were not working.

It was then that he noticed an under-sized idiot boy standing a little way apart from the grooms.

One of them passed him and he said something, pointing with his finger and trying with his other hand to hold on to the groom as if to make him listen.

"Who is that?" Lord Vernham asked the Headgroom.

"That be Loony Billy, M'Lord. He comes up here from the village to look at t'horses and we can't keep him away. Some o' the lads are sorry for him because the village children tease him unmerciful.'

Lord Vernham looked indifferently towards the idiot, then catching a word of what he was saying walked towards him.

"Tell me what you said just then, Billy," he asked quietly.

For a moment it seemed as if Billy found it impossible to reply.

He looked at Lord Vernham in a frightened manner. Then mouthing his words with difficulty he said:

"C-cat . . . big c-cat!"

"Where did you see a big cat?" Lord Vernham asked.

Again Billy pointed across the stable-yard and now Lord Vernham said gently:

"Show me, Billy, show me where you saw the cat go."

It seemed to take the loony a moment to realize what was required of him. Then he set off, walking slowly and unsteadily because one of his legs was shorter than the other, towards a gap between the buildings.

Lord Vernham followed him while everybody else in the stable-yard stood still and silent.

"Show me where the big cat went," Lord Vernham insisted when they came to the tall grass. Billy pointed into the centre of it.

It only took Lord Vernham a few seconds once he had seen the hole to realize what had happened.

He could not only see the broken ladder but he could also hear Bobo whining below in the darkness.

He gave a shout and the grooms came running.

"I want a lantern and strong ropes quickly!" he ordered.

The stable-lads ran to obey him and turning to the Head-groom Lord Vernham asked:

"Is there water in this well?"

"I don't rightly know, M'Lord. I've not seen it before. We've not had time to do anything since we arrived but clean out the stables for the horses—they was in a terrible state!"

"I understand," Lord Vernham replied.

He waited impatiently until a lantern was brought to him.

He tied it to a string and, letting it down the well, he lay on the edge looking below.

It was not easy to discern anything very clearly, but he thought he saw a glimmer of white and realised that in fact the well was not very deep.

As soon as the ropes arrived he made the Head-

groom hold the lantern on one side of the well and
the rest let him down very slowly on thick ropes.

He had to remove the ladder when he was halfway
down from where it had fallen to wedge itself against
the brick wall on the other side.

This was not difficult, but it meant another rope
being lowered for it to be hauled away before he could
proceed further.

Lord Vernham told them to drop him still lower
and as the lantern descended with him he had his first
sight of Jarita.

She was lying sprawled out on her back as she must
have fallen, her eyes closed, her arms flung wide.

Nestling against her was Bobo, giving tiny growls
and plaintive whines because he was frightened.

When Lord Vernham found his feet on the bottom
of the well he realised that by the greatest good
fortune it was covered with a thick layer of dried
leaves and grasses.

Both Bobo and Jarita had fallen some considerable
height, but there was nothing rough or hard to break
their bones.

Bobo anyway would have fallen naturally on his
feet, since a lion is a born acrobat, but it was different
for Jarita.

She had been knocked unconscious but as far as
Lord Vernham could see by the light of the flickering
lantern she was not wounded and neither her legs nor
her arms were fractured.

He shouted for a rope, his voice echoing eerily
round the confined space. Then he took off his cravat
and wrapped it round Bobo's body so that the rope
would not hurt him.

The men hauled up the cub and now Lord Vernham
could turn his attention to Jarita.

Very gently he lifted her in his arms, knowing that
she was so light that the ropes which held him could
haul them up together.

He held her close against him and her head rested against his shoulder.

He looked down at her, wondering why she was still unconscious and hoping she would not suffer from a bad concussion.

As he did so he suddenly realised that he had a wild, almost uncontrollable desire to kiss her lips.

For a moment he could hardly believe the sensation that swept over him.

His heart was thumping against his chest, his breath came quicker, there was a constriction in his throat, and he knew that what he felt for her was quite different from anything he had felt before.

Instinctively his arms tightened to draw her a little closer and he knew in that moment that he was in love.

It was so unexpected—so astonishing—that the knowledge took his breath away.

After his first feeling of antagonism for Jarita had been changed to pity and compassion, he had only thought of her as a wild creature who needed his protection and help.

Now he could hardly credit that he was not imagining the emotion which possessed him.

Then with a twist of his lips he thought:

'What an extraordinary place in which to fall in love!'

He looked up to the light above him.

"Pull me up!" he ordered. "And do it slowly and very carefully."

The stable-hands obeyed and a minute or so later their hands reached down to haul him and Jarita into the sunshine.

"Shall I take Her Ladyship?" the Head-groom enquired.

"No," Lord Vernham replied. "Unfasten the ropes. I will carry her myself."

Before he walked towards the house he told them to reward Billy.

"Give the boy plenty to eat and a shilling."

He knew that it would be folly to give an idiot lad more, as it would only be taken from him in the village, but as if he felt he had not been very generous he added:

"Let the boy come here as often as he wishes."

Then he walked away, carrying Jarita in his arms as if she was very precious.

When they reached the Abbey he carried her up the stairs, sending a footman running ahead for Mrs. Williams.

He walked into Jarita's bed-room, looking into her face and yearning to awaken her with a kiss.

Her eyes were still closed, the lashes very dark against her pale cheeks.

"I have searched the whole world for you," Lord Vernham said in his heart.

Then as Mrs. Williams came into the room he laid Jarita gently back against the lace-edged pillows.

\* \* \*

Jarita thought she was at the end of a long, dark tunnel.

She was moving, although she was not quite certain how, towards a flicker of light. She opened her eyes and realized that the light came from the candles by her bed.

Vaguely she wondered why she had gone to sleep without blowing them out.

Then as she gazed at the canopy over her head and the silk curtains falling from it there was a rustling sound and Mrs. Williams's voice saying:

"Are you awake, M'Lady?"

With difficulty Jarita focussed her eyes on the House-keeper's face and realised she was looking very anxious.

She wanted to answer but her mouth felt too dry.

Mrs. Williams put a hand behind her head, lifted her gently, and held a cup to her lips.

Jarita drank gratefully. She thought she must have been thirsty for a very long time.

There was the sound of a door opening.

"I think Her Ladyships regained consciousness, M'Lord," Mrs. Williams said in a whisper.

She moved from Jarita's side as she spoke and Jarita looked up into her husband's face.

"How do you feel?" he asked.

She felt his hand cover hers and her fingers held on to his.

"I . . . fell . . ." she managed to say.

"You fell into the well," he replied, "when you were trying to save Bobo."

"Bo . . . bo?"

He saw the question in her eyes.

"There is nothing wrong with him," he answered, "and he is driving Holden crazy; so the sooner you get well enough to look after him again, the better!"

Jarita wanted to laugh but it was impossible.

"I am . . . not . . . hurt?"

Lord Vernham shook his head.

"The Doctor says there are no bones broken. You had a slight concussion from the fall. I expect it was very frightening, but after a day or so in bed you will be perfectly all right again."

"I do not . . . want to . . . stay in bed," Jarita said petulantly.

"Kingfisher misses you," Lord Vernham said, and saw the light in her eyes.

" I was . . . going riding with . . . you."

"We both missed our ride yesterday."

"Yesterday?"

"You woke up last night, but you were not making sense. Everybody is a little delirious after being concussed. It is not important."

He was trying to reassure her, Jarita knew, but she

was disappointed that she had not only missed her ride yesterday with him, but again today.

"I . . . want to get . . . well . . . quickly."

"That is what I want you to do," he said. "We all miss you."

He realized that Mrs. Williams had tactfully withdrawn from the room. His hands still held Jarita's as he said softly:

"I had no idea that the absence of one small woman could make a house like this seem so empty or so quiet."

"Quiet?"

He knew she was thinking of the noise the workmen were making and his eyes were on hers as he said:

"Quiet in the way which matters. I have nobody to talk to at meals and last evening there was so much I was unable to discuss. I also needed your advice."

"You . . . really . . . miss me?"

"Much more than I can tell you at this moment," he answered.

She gave a little sigh.

"I do not think . . . anyone has ever . . . missed me before."

"And now there are quite a lot of people waiting for you to come back to them."

He smiled as he continued:

"There is Bobo, of course, and I am sure he is being so naughty and so destructive simply because he cannot understand why you are not there. There is Kingfisher, who is waiting for his carrots, and there is—me."

It seemed to Jarita there was a special significance in the last word. Then she told herself he was only being polite.

When he had so much to do, so many things to occupy him, it was unlikely that he really missed her, and yet she wanted to believe what he said.

"You do such unpredictable things that I think in

future I shall have to use the same chains on you as we are using on Scobi and Meena," Lord Vernham said with a smile.

"How did they . . . work?" Jarita enquired.

"Better than I ever imagined they would," he replied. "Cheetahs, as you know, are very intelligent. I think they have reasoned that if this is the only way in which they can be exercised, they will accept it rather than stay cooped up in their enclosure."

He added:

"There was only one difficult moment when a hare got up in front of Meena. She sprang at it and very nearly pulled me out of the saddle! I managed to hold her but she looked at me reproachfully, not understanding why she was not allowed to catch a good meal when she saw one!"

This time Jarita managed to chuckle.

"I am going to leave you now," Lord Vernham said. "Go to sleep and if the Doctor is pleased with you when he comes in the morning, I will allow you a visitor in the shape of Bobo."

"And . . . you will come and . . . see me, too?"

"You may be sure of that," he promised.

In his own bed-room he stood for a long time at the open window looking out into the garden.

How could he have imagined six months ago in Africa that he would find himself here at the Abbey, the owner of it for his lifetime, possessor of a title which he never thought would be his—and married.

He remembered how furiously he had loathed the thought of a wife when his uncle had told him his position as regarded the Abbey and the great debt that was owed to Theobold Muir.

He recalled the rebellious feelings which had possessed him when he was waiting for Jarita to come up the aisle on her father's arm.

He had loathed Theobold Muir with a hatred which he had tried to tell himself was unreasonable and due only to his personal dislike of being under obligation to a stranger.

But he had known when he saw Jarita's scarred back that his hatred had been based on the same instinct that guided him when he assessed a man's character or trained an animal to obey him by the use of his own senses.

Yet now he loved Theobold Muir's daughter in a way that he had never loved a woman before.

Looking back, he realised that women had always made the first advances to him. They had always made it very clear that they desired him and that he had for them an irresistible attraction.

Jarita was different.

While she had begun to trust him he was well aware that one unwary move, one ill-chosen word, could frighten her again and she would shrink from him as she had done the day of their marriage.

"I have a long way to go before she will love me as I love her," Lord Vernham told himself, looking out into the darkness.

At the same time, he thought as he watched the moon rising over the lake and the stars glittering over the trees that the beauty of the Abbey was as perfect and ethereal as Jarita was herself.

He had never known a woman to have such expressive eyes nor had he experienced anything in his whole life as fascinating as watching the expression of fear on her face change into one of trust.

"One day she will love me," he vowed.

He thought that while their relationship at present was as he had wanted it to be, just friendship, it would be impossible for a woman with those red lights in her hair not to have the fires of passion somewhere within her, dormant, unawakened.

It would be a fascination as well as a rapture to awaken her to the wonder of desire, to arouse her one day to the first stirrings of passion, to teach her the ecstasy of loving and being loved.

Lord Vernham sighed and it seemed to come from the very depths of his being.

'I have never felt like this before,' he thought again.

Everything round him had a kind of dream-like quality because it was so unexpected, and yet so beautiful.

And although he had been unaware of it, it was exactly what he had always wanted.

"Mine! Mine!" he said aloud.

He was looking into the sleeping garden, but his thoughts were really with the woman who was asleep next door, so near and yet divided by a closed door.

\*    \*    \*

Two days later Jarita came downstairs followed by an excited Bobo, who paused a little apprehensively before he negotiated each step, but was determined not to be left behind.

"Let me carry him," Jarita begged Lord Vernham.

"He is quite capable of walking on his own four feet," he replied, "but I am not so certain that you are steady on yours."

"I feel completely well, and I will not be mollycoddled," she protested.

She found, however, that it was delightful to be lifted by him onto a chair on the terrace with her feet resting on a stool and her legs covered by a light rug.

There was the fragrance of the lilac and syringa, the first buds were appearing on the rose trees, and the sun was warm.

"I am so happy," she said.

"That is what I want you to be," Lord Vernham answered, "and we are going to celebrate your return to civilisation with a glass of champagne."

A footman came onto the terrace as he spoke and Jarita took a glass from the tray he offered. When the flunkey had left, Lord Vernham said:

"I want to drink a toast to my wife."

There was something in the way he spoke and the look in his eyes which made Jarita feel shy.

"I ought really to be drinking to you," she replied, "because you were clever enough to rescue me."

"I cannot take the credit," Lord Vernham answered. "It was Billy who did that."

"Billy?"

He told her about the loony boy and after a moment she said:

"Could we do . . . something for him?"

"I have already enquired if it is possible," Lord Vernham said.

She gave him a quick glance.

"I might have . . . guessed you would do that."

"I have had him examined by our Doctor," he went on, "who thinks his brain must have been injured at birth."

"So it is a hopeless case?"

"I am afraid so, but I have arranged that he shall be better fed in future and have given his parents some money so that they can look after him properly."

Jarita gave a little sigh.

"I never realised there could be anyone in the world as . . . kind as . . . you."

"There are lots of people," Lord Vernham protested, "it is just that you have never met them."

"Yesterday when I was alone I thought how . . . different everything might have . . . been if I had had to . . . marry your cousin . . . Gervaise."

"Forget him!" Lord Vernham said sharply. "I do not wish you even to think of him."

"I was only being grateful because you were so . . . different, as you said you . . . were. I did not believe you at . . . first."

"And now?"

"I know that you are very different in every way from

any man I have ever known or imagined existed in the whole world."

There was a little throb in her voice which Lord Vernham did not miss and he bent forward to take her hand in his.

"I am not only glad you think me different," he said, "but I am very glad that you think about me at all."

He raised her hand to his lips and kissed it.

He felt her stiffen for a moment as if in surprise. Then instead of drawing her hand away she held on to him.

"You do not think that you will become . . . bored here . . . and want to . . . go to London?"

Lord Vernham looked at her in surprise.

"Why should you imagine that?"

She looked away from him, but he was sure there was a worried expression in her eyes.

"Papa said once that a man must always have new things to interest him, that his brain is not content unless it is stimulated. I was wondering . . . if the Abbey and even the . . . animals would be enough."

"There is something else here which interests me very much," Lord Vernham said, "something I find very stimulating which I fancy will enthrall me for a very long time."

"What is that?" Jarita asked curiously.

"You!"

For a second she looked at him as if she thought he might be teasing her. Then when she realised he was serious the colour rose in her cheeks.

"We said we would be friends, Jarita," Lord Vernham said, "and let me tell you that friends not only stimulate each other's brain but they also forge bonds which make everything they do together seem to be of special interest, or if you like, a special excitement."

"You feel . . . that about . . . me?"

The words were spoken in such a low voice that he could hardly hear them.

"I enjoy everything we do together, and more than anything else I enjoy being with you," Lord Vernham said.

He kissed her hand again as he spoke, then rose to his feet and walked to the balustrade of the terrace as if he was interested in something on the lake below them.

He knew, although she would not say so, that she wanted him to go on talking to her and that she was intrigued and a little thrilled by what he had just said.

Lord Vernham's long experience of wild animals had taught him that the best way to attract an animal was to pay no attention to it or to walk away.

He was astute enough in his pursuit of Jarita to realise that where she was concerned he had to arouse in her a yearning for his company, a desire to listen to what he had to say about their personal relationship.

With an effort because even to be close to her made him long almost uncontrollably to put his arms round her, he managed to say:

"I wonder if Bella has ever missed Bobo? Lions are strange animals: they are devoted mothers in the way that they feed their young for two years and fight valiantly against overwhelming odds to protect them. But when a cub dies it never seems to perturb them unduly."

Bobo was sitting beside Jarita's chair and she bent down to pick him up in her arms.

"I should miss Bobo . . . I should miss him terribly if he died or was taken away from me."

She put her cheek as she spoke against Bobo's soft, furry head.

Lord Vernham did not reply and after a moment she asked:

"Would you not miss him, too?"

"Not half as much as I would miss you if you left me," he replied.

He did not turn round as he spoke, but he had a

feeling that Jarita's eyes, widening questioningly, were
on his back.

* * *

The sun that had shone all the afternoon was over-
cast in the early evening and dark clouds covered the
sky. It was warm and airless.

Mrs. Williams, as she put Jarita to bed, predicted
there would be a thunder-storm.

"Real bad they can be round here, M'Lady," she
said, "and many's the time I've wondered if the Abbey
itself would be struck. Perhaps there's a special bless-
ing attached to the building though, because it's always
survived them."

"I do not like thunder and lightning," Jarita replied.
"One of our chimney-pots was struck once at home. It
was very frightening."

"I'm sure it was, M'Lady, but you needn't worry
about that happening here. Shall I blow out the candles?"

"Yes, please."

Jarita was hoping that Lord Vernham would come
and say good-night to her, but she did not really expect
that he would because he had said good-night when he
had taken her upstairs before dinner.

"You must have something light to eat and go to
sleep," he commanded.

"I am well, and I am not in the least tired," Jarita
replied.

"You must obey the Doctor's orders," he said firmly.
"Tomorrow, if you are very good and promise you will
not overtire yourself, you can stay up for dinner."

"You do not seem to realise that I am as tough as
any of your lions!"

"But not as swift as the cheetahs," he teased, "or
as noisy as the parrots."

Jarita laughed, she could not help it.

Horatio had been using very bad language at the

footmen in the Hall and the Butler had complained that it would be impossible to keep discipline if the bird stayed there.

"They cannot help laughing," Lord Vernham told Jarita when he related what had been said. "Personally, I think it brings a nice air of informality to the Abbey, which has often been sadly lacking in the past."

"I love to hear him," she smiled.

"Then I shall listen to no more arguments about Horatio being taken away," Lord Vernham answered.

She gave him a grateful little smile.

'He is so kind, so very kind,' Jarita thought. Then because she was in fact rather tired, although she would not admit it, she fell asleep.

*   *   *

Lord Vernham, although he did not sleep for a long time, was awakened by a violent clap of thunder and by the lightning which flashed through the open windows of his bed-room.

It reminded him of the storms he had endured in Africa, but now he had a substantial roof over his head and a floor beneath his feet.

He had often been woken up to find himself in a collapsed, sodden tent or to see all his belongings floating on a stream caused by the torrential rain.

The rain was only just starting outside but he knew that when it did come it would splash in through the windows and doubtless make a mess on the floor.

He therefore rose to close the casements and as he did so the connecting door between his room and Jarita's opened.

"B-Bobo's . . . frightened."

There was a little tremor in her voice which made Lord Vernham ask:

"And you?"

"I am . . . too," she admitted. "It is very . . . noisy."

As she spoke a clap of thunder right overhead ob-
literated her voice.

Lord Vernham fastened the window and turned to
see her in the candlelight standing in her white nightgown with her fair hair streaming over her shoulders
and Bobo in her arms.

She looked so lovely that he drew in his breath and
only with the greatest difficulty prevented himself from
walking towards her and pulling her against him.

"We will get Bobo a bottle," he said.

"There is one in my room," Jarita answered.
"Holden brought it to me a quarter of an hour ago, and
he will not touch it . . . he is too afraid."

Bobo, hiding his face against her, was whining
piteously, his little body shaking with fear.

"I will see what I can do," Lord Vernham said. "Sit
on the bed—or better still, get into it. I will fetch the
bottle."

He walked from the room as he spoke to come back
a moment later with the bottle in his hands.

It was still warm and he sat down on the edge of the
mattress, facing Jarita, who had propped herself against
his pillows and was stroking Bobo.

Another crash of thunder startled her and she looked
apprehensively at Lord Vernham.

"Give him to me," he said quietly. "I think the fact
that you too are frightened increases his own fears."

He took the cub from her as he spoke.

"It is stupid of me," Jarita said, "but because I was
frightened of thunder when I was a little girl, Papa, to
teach me to be brave, would not allow me to have a
night-light but made me stay alone in my bed-room
with the curtains drawn back."

The more he heard about Theobold Muir the more
he loathed him, Lord Vernham thought.

But he said nothing as he tried to persuade Bobo to
suck his bottle, only to fail as Jarita had done.

Finally he put the cub down on the floor and it instantly disappeared under the flounce of the bed.

"He will be happier there," Lord Vernham said. "Wild animals always feel they are protected when they are underneath something low. That is why Bella hides her cubs in the shrubs and in the jungle they will creep underneath a rock or into a cave."

He was looking at Jarita as he spoke. He felt the blood throbbing in his temples and his heart beating wildly. But he knew it was only because she trusted him that she was unself-conscious.

Through the thin lawn of her nightgown he could see the soft outline of her breasts and he thought no woman could look more pure and innocent and at the same time utterly desirable.

Her hair was glinting in the light of the candles, and her eyes were wide and frightened in her small face.

Another crash of thunder seemed to reverberate in the room and now as if she could not help it, Jarita reached out towards Lord Vernham and instantly his arms were round her and he was holding her close against him.

She hid her face against his shoulder and he could feel that she was trembling. But not in the same way she had trembled on the night they were married.

She was afraid but it was entirely a physical emotion and not mental as it had been when she tried to drown herself.

"You are quite safe," he said, hoping his voice sounded calmer than he felt.

It was a joy and at the same time an agony to hold her so close. Her hair smelt of flowers and he could feel the soft silkiness of it against his lips.

His heart was hammering in his breast and he wondered if she would be aware of it.

Now the rain was coming down in a downpour that had almost a tropical strength.

"The thunder-storm is passing," Lord Vernham said.

But he hoped as he spoke that it would linger on so that he could contrive to hold Jarita close to him.

The next clap of thunder was considerably further away and after a moment she raised her head.

"It is . . . leaving and we are . . . safe," she murmured.

"Quite safe," he answered.

She moved and instantly he released her.

"I . . . I am ashamed of myself."

"There is no need to be."

"I knew I would . . . feel safe with you."

"That is what husbands are for—among other things."

The last words were an afterthought and she wondered if she should ask him what he meant.

"I . . . I must go back to my own room," she said after a moment.

"There is no hurry," he answered.

He wondered what she would say if he begged her to stay, if he told her that he wanted more than anything in the world to hold her in his arms all night, to kiss her and make love to her, to make her his in reality and not only in name.

Then as the very words trembled on his lips, as he felt his whole being surge out in a passionate, almost uncontrollable desire to possess her, he told himself it was too soon.

The fear that had made her try to kill herself had changed to friendship, but some of it still lingered beneath the surface—he was sure of that.

He dared not risk losing her confidence now. He dared not destroy the trust she already had in him.

In a voice which sounded strangely unlike his own, Lord Vernham said:

"I want you to have a good night. We have a lot to do tomorrow. If you think you can sleep I will take you back to your own room."

"The storm has almost passed, and the thunder has gone," Jarita replied.

She listened as she spoke and now it was difficult to hear the last rumble in the far distance.

"If you are afraid—come back to me."

"I do not wish to disturb you," she answered. "I would not have come had I not seen a light beneath your door."

"I would like to think that you would have come anyhow, because you were frightened and knew I would protect you."

"I knew that . . . too."

"You know I am always there waiting for you if you want me," Lord Vernham said slowly.

She looked into his eyes and suddenly was very still.

There was a depth in his voice and an expression on his face she could not put into words.

She felt as if something strange happened inside her and her heart was beating rather quickly.

She looked away from him shyly.

"What about Bobo . . . will he come with . . . me?"

"Try going without him," Lord Vernham suggested.

Jarita got out of bed. As she did so she was silhouetted against the candlelight and he could see the curves of her slim body through the thin muslin of her nightgown.

He drew in his breath, aware that once again the blood was throbbing in his temples and there was a fire rising within him. Without meaning to do so he clenched his hands.

He watched Jarita walk towards the door.

Only as she opened it was there a movement beneath the bed and a small ball of fur rushed from under the valance and crossed the carpet towards her.

"He came after me!' Jarita cried with a note of triumph in her voice.

Lord Vernham as he rose slowly to his feet told himself it was a good omen for the future.

# Chapter Six

Jarita hurried into the Breakfast-Room carrying a parcel in her arms.

When she saw Lord Vernham seated at the table she exclaimed:

"Oh, I had hoped to be down first!"

He rose to his feet, smiling at her, and she walked towards him to say shyly:

"Many happy returns of the day! Here is a present for you!"

"A present for me?" he repeated in surprise. "How did you know it was my birthday?"

"Mrs. Williams told me," she answered, "so I have made you something which I hope you will like."

Lord Vernham opened the present and saw it was a pair of black velvet slippers skilfully embroidered with his monogram surmounted by a coronet.

The embroidery was in gold thread and was very effective.

"You worked this yourself?" he asked.

"Yes," she answered. "It was difficult to prevent you from seeing me doing it. I wanted my gift to be a surprise."

"It is a very big surprise!" he answered. "And thank

128

you very much, Jarita. I have not received a present for many years."

"And you like them . . . you really like them?" she asked anxiously.

"I shall feel very grand and opulent in them," he answered, "and I shall treasure them because you made them for me yourself."

There was something in the way he spoke which made her drop her eyes.

She had in fact taken a great deal of trouble over the slippers. Holden had bought them knowing Lord Vernham's size, and Mrs. Williams had shown her how to use the gold thread.

Jarita had always been able to embroider well but she had never attempted anything for a man before and she had been half-afraid that Lord Vernham would think they were too ostentatious.

"I thought I was too old to remember my birthday," he was saying, "but you have made it a very special occasion."

"You must be careful not to let Bobo eat your slippers," Jarita warned. "Mrs. Williams locks all my shoes away in the wardrobe or else places them on a chair. Bobo is getting more destructive every day."

"He is practising for the time when he can kill his own food," Lord Vernham said, "but I assure you I will keep my very beautiful birthday-present out of his reach."

Jarita sat down at the table and a footman came into the room with more silver dishes.

"Now we have to decide how we can celebrate this auspicious occasion," Lord Vernham said. "I had thought that we might exercise the cheetahs this morning and inspect one of the farms at the same time, but you may wish to do something else."

"I would like that above everything," Jarita replied, "and it is your birthday . . . not mine."

"We will have a special celebration when yours

comes round," he promised, "and I shall have to try to rival your present. But I cannot think of anything I can make for you."

"There are so many things one can give a woman," Jarita answered, "but men are far more difficult."

"I think when you know me better you will find there are a great many things I want," he answered, "especially from you."

She looked at him questioningly as if she did not understand quite what he meant, but he began to talk of other things. As soon as breakfast was finished they set off to ride across the Park, each of them holding a cheetah on its long chain.

There was a great deal to see when they reached the farm and it was luncheon-time when they returned to the Abbey.

During the meal Lord Vernham realised that the Chef had made a special effort, obviously on Jarita's instructions, and afterwards they went out on the terrace.

There were two rest-chairs side by side, and having arranged Jarita in hers Lord Vernham had just thrown himself down in the other when a footman appeared with a note on a silver salver.

"What can this be?" he asked.

He read it and Jarita saw there was a frown between his eyes.

"What has happened? What is wrong?" she asked.

"It is annoying," he replied, "but this is from the foreman who is supervising the renovations at North Farm. One of the main walls of the house has collapsed, owing, he says, to damp and neglect. It means I shall have to go and see what can be done about it."

"Shall I come with you?"

Lord Vernham hesitated for a moment, then he answered:

"I think if you are honest you will admit you have

done enough riding for today. I will go alone, it will be quicker, and I will be back as soon as possible."

She was disappointed. At the same time, she did feel a little tired.

Although it was now nearly a week since she had fallen into the well, there were still bruises on her back, replacing those which had now faded from the beating which her father had given her.

"Order Black Knight to be brought round in ten minutes," Lord Vernham said to the footman.

"Very good, M'Lord."

Jarita knew that Black Knight was the fastest horse in the stable.

He was a new acquisition and it would be unlikely, if she went with Lord Vernham, that her horse would be able to keep up with the speed and endurance of Black Knight.

What was more, it would be impossible to ride Kingfisher after he had already been fully exercised before luncheon.

"I will stay here," she said with a little sigh, but her eyes were very expressive.

"When I come back I am going to read you a love story about two elephants," Lord Vernham said.

"Two elephants?" Jarita exclaimed.

"It is a story I have written myself from the tale that has been told by animal-lovers for some years."

"You have written it?"

Lord Vernham smiled.

"I have a secret to tell you. I have been thinking of writing a book about animals for some time."

"How exciting!" Jarita said. "I would love you to read it to me."

"I have not quite finished it yet. There are so many fascinating stories of animals' devotion to each other which I am sure should be written down and might perhaps make people understand them a little better."

He paused, then he said:

"I thought in fact it would be something we could do together."

"That is the most exciting thing anyone has ever said to me!" Jarita said. "Oh, please, hurry back and read to me about the elephants."

"Their names were Hans and Parki," Lord Vernham said, "and they loved each other so deeply that when Hans died Parki went into a decline and there is no doubt that when a year later in 1805 she died too, it was of a broken heart."

"I want to hear all about them."

"Then I shall hurry because I know you are waiting for me."

Lord Vernham took her hand as he spoke and kissed it. When he raised his head he looked into her eyes and she felt, although he did not speak, that he was trying to tell her something.

She could not guess what it was, but she felt strangely excited.

When he was gone she was alone on the terrace with Bobo, who had been asleep under her chair, and she cuddled him in her arms.

He was growing much bigger and although his head and paws were still large in proportion to his body he was extremely attractive.

He had a habit when Jarita was talking to him of putting his head on one side and apparently listening to her, which she found quite entrancing.

"I wish we could have gone with him, Bobo," she said a little wistfully.

Bobo considered this for some moments, then tried to eat the buttons off her gown.

She prevented him from doing it by turning him over on his back and rubbing his tummy, which he loved.

"I spoil you," she said to him. "You are getting too big for me to make so much fuss of you. Soon you will have to look after yourself."

But Bobo was still young enough to tire quickly and

soon he fell asleep on Jarita's lap and she stroked him gently while she was deep in her thoughts.

She was in fact thinking of Lord Vernham and wondering if he would be pleased with the birthday-cake she had told the Chef to bake for him.

If he had not had a present for so many years, then he would certainly not have had a birthday-cake either!

She heard one of the footmen come out onto the terrace.

"Mr. Theobold Muir, M'Lady!" he announced.

Startled, Jarita turned her head and saw her father moving towards her.

"Good-afternoon, Jarita. I understand you are alone. This is excellent! It gives us an opportunity to talk together."

"I did not . . . expect to . . . see you . . . Papa."

Jarita would have risen but he put his hand on her shoulder.

"Do not get up," he said. "I can see you are very comfortable, despite the creature you have on your lap."

"It is a lion cub, Papa."

"I am aware of that. Your husband told me he intended to keep a menagerie here at the Abbey, but I did not expect he would actually have wild animals in the house."

"Bobo is very young and we had to hand-rear him, otherwise he would have died."

"You know my feelings as regards pets," Theobold Muir said coldly. "I do not intend to waste my time discussing them, but rather to talk to you about yourself, Jarita."

"About . . . me?"

"I have some interesting news for you."

"What is that?"

"I have just come from London, where I have been supervising the redecoration and refurnishing of Vernham House."

She looked at him in surprise.

"I did not know there was one."

"It was where the last Lord Vernham and his son lived when they were not at the Abbey. Actually it was not entailed and I bought it from them some years ago, but it needed a lot doing to it."

Jarita was silent and after a moment Theobold Muir said:

"I have been thinking of your future, Jarita, and while I was renovating Vernham House I thought that you and I could have some very interesting times there together."

Jarita looked at him with a puzzled expression on her face.

"I do . . . not think I understand Papa . . . Alvaric does not . . . like London."

"That I can understand," Theobold Muir said. "He has always lived abroad, and that is doubtless where his interests still lie."

"I think, Papa . . ." Jarita said hesitatingly, "my husband's interests are here. He l-loves the . . . Abbey."

She looked at her father as she spoke and thought there was a smile of disbelief on his face.

"My dear Jarita," he replied. "You are very young and naïve. Of course your husband is pleased with the Abbey for the moment. What man would not enjoy spending enormous sums of money on restoring it to its former magnificence—but have you ever considered what will happen when it is finished?"

He did not wait for Jarita to answer but went on:

"Once everything is complete and he has an heir, I am quite certain my son-in-law will wish to go abroad again. Once an explorer and an adventurer—always an explorer and an adventurer. And Vernham will be no exception!"

"Are you saying that he will . . . leave me?"

"Not legally, my dear," Theobold Muir replied. "He will doubtless return from time to time to give you an-

other child and make certain he has plenty of sons to
take his place when he dies."

Theobold Muir's eyes narrowed as he said:

"His uncle made the unfortunate mistake of having
only one. I cannot believe that your husband will be so
stupid as to endanger the succession another time."

He did not look at his daughter as he spoke or he
would have seen the look of horror and fear in Jarita's
large eyes.

"What I am going to suggest," Theobold Muir said,
"is that when this happens you will take your rightful
place as a leader of Society. I will be with you to help
and guide you, and I think in the magnificent Reception Rooms at Vernham House we could create a Salon
where the best intellects of Society would be pleased to
gather."

As always when her father talked to her, Jarita felt
as if he sapped her will to think for herself.

She felt almost as if she was mesmerised by him,
while what he was saying was so terrifying that she
could feel it encroaching upon her almost as though it
would happen tomorrow.

"There are men I have always wanted to meet and
talk to," Theobold Muir was saying, "but I have not
had the opportunity of making their acquaintance because they have not admitted me to their more intimate
circles."

There was just a touch of excitement in his voice as
he went on:

"Well, that can easily be remedied when you and I
are in residence at Vernham House."

"B-but, Papa, I do not want to go to . . . London . . .
and I do not believe that Alvaric will leave here . . . or
me."

Theobold Muir turned to look at her and she saw
the contempt in his expression.

"Do you really believe you can hold a man like that

at your side for long?" he asked. "What have you to offer him except your money—which is already his?"

He laughed and it was an unpleasant sound.

"All the Vernes are attracted by and have an attraction for women, and I can easily imagine the exotic birds-of-Paradise with whom your husband associated in the East."

ᐟ Jarita made a little murmur of horror and he said cruelly:

"I saw the expression on Vernham's face on your wedding-day and I knew before, when I insisted that he had to marry you or let the Abbey decay into ruin, that the idea of marriage appalled him. Face facts, Jarita, or rather, leave everything to me and I will look after you as I have always done."

Jarita felt as if he were crushing her and it was impossible to fight against him.

A picture of what he was saying flashed before her eyes. She could almost see Alvaric leaving her, going abroad, perhaps taking his animals with him because they would be lonely and unhappy without him.

And she would be left behind.

He would not want her if, as her father suggested, he was returning to the beautiful foreign women who attracted him and whom doubtless he loved.

Somehow she had never thought of him being concerned with women until this moment.

Now she realised how stupid and ignorant she had been not to realise that any man of Alvaric's age, who was so handsome, strong, and attractive, would not have had innumerable women in his life.

He seemed genuinely to want her to be his friend. But he had not offered her love, and after all, as her father had said, why should he love her?

He had loathed and resented the idea of being married even as she had, and she supposed that he had treated her as he had only because he was a kind person and realised she was in need of kindness.

"You are a married woman now," Theobold Muir said. "I do not have to speak to you as if you were a stupid, ignorant girl. You have to face life as it is and not as it appears in some trashy, romantic novelette."

He paused before he continued:

"Vernham will leave you to your own devices in perhaps a year's time and you will then have to make a life of your own. What I am suggesting will prove extremely interesting and will open to us all the doors that have always been closed in the past."

He was speaking with a note in his voice which Jarita recognised.

It was something that had always been there when he talked to her of being the Mistress of Vernham Abbey, becoming a Lady of Title, and making the important marriage he visualised for her.

Now, having attained his first objective, he wanted to go further.

She could see all too clearly the type of life he envisaged they would lead in London, the glittering parties and Assemblies they would attend, the huge Receptions they would give at which, shy and frightened, she would have to play hostess.

Every instinct in her mind and body cried out against it; and yet she asked herself whether, if what her father predicted came true, and she was completely alone, she could bear to stay at the Abbey without Alvaric, and without even Bobo to console her.

Then her brain told her there was one saving grace in what her father planned.

He had said her husband would not leave her until she had produced an heir, and at the moment at any rate there was no chance of her doing that!

Jarita's misery lightened. After all there was a light, if only a faint one in the darkness.

Almost as if he sensed what she was thinking, Theobold Muir said:

"Of course there is no immediate hurry. It would be

impossible for this to happen before next year. Are you with child?"

The question seemed to Jarita almost like a pistol-shot.

Because she was far too frightened to tell him the truth, she merely dropped her eyes, while the colour rose in her cheeks.

"It is too soon to be certain," he said. "But you had best make sure there is an heir to inherit this place. What is being done to it has certainly cost you a great deal of money."

"It is . . . Alvaric's money now."

Jarita's voice was very low, but it was defiant.

Theobold Muir laughed.

"Being a Vernham, he has made sure of that! But I can provide you with anything you need personally, and if it concerns my plans for our future I will write you a cheque for any sum you ask of me."

Jarita knew he expected her to express her gratitude, but the words would not come to her lips.

As if he wished to find fault, her father said sharply:

"Surely you realise by this time, Jarita, that you should have offered me some sort of refreshment? I see there is a bell by your side. I suggest you ring it."

"Y-yes . . . Papa, of course, I am . . . sorry!"

She rang the little gold bell which stood on a table beside her chair and almost instantly a footman appeared.

"What would you like to drink?" she asked her father.

"I never drink anything in the middle of the day except champagne," Theobold Muir replied.

Father and daughter sat in silence until within a few moments the Butler came onto the terrace with two footmen, one carrying a tray on which reposed the glasses, the other the wine-cooler in which there stood a bottle of champagne.

Jarita realised that this must have been ready before

she sent for it, and she thought how remiss she had been in not offering her first visitor some refreshment as might have been expected.

But within herself she was crying out at the idea of being hostess to her father in London and having to fulfill the role he expected of her.

How could she do such a thing? How indeed could she contemplate a future without Alvaric, without his kindness, his consideration, his friendship?

Then the women whom her father had conjured up seemed to appear so vividly before her eyes that she could almost see them; women very unlike herself, with long dark hair and huge liquid eyes, beautiful, voluptuous, and inviting.

How was it possible, when he had them, that he could be interested even for a moment in someone as small, insignificant, and timorous as herself?

'But I have been so happy,' she thought, 'so happy these last few days that I had forgotten what it was like to be afraid and uncertain.'

Just as he had done before her marriage, her father seemed again to menace her and to enforce her obedience to the point where she was too frightened to rebel against him.

Because she had done it once, because she had run away in her fear of being married, the whole agony she had suffered when he beat her swept over her.

It was the terror not only of the physical pain but of the mental humiliation, and it was so intense that she felt sick and on the verge of fainting.

She could hear again her own sobs after someone, she supposed it was her father, carried her unconscious to her bed-room and flung her down on the bed.

She was then past screaming; she could only cry and go on crying until Miss Dawson had given her something to make her sleep, and even then she had dreamt that she was in tears and awoke to find it was the truth.

"I cannot fight against Papa," she told herself now.

She dared not even look at him as he sat beside her, sipping the champagne with a half-smile on his face that made him seem more sinister and frightening than when he was angry.

He drained his glass and set it down on the table before he rose to his feet.

"I will leave you now, Jarita," he said. "Think about what I have told you because you must continue with your studies. Do not let your French get rusty: French is very important to a political hostess. And keep up with day-to-day events. You take the *Times* and the *Morning Post* I presume?"

"I . . . I think . . . so," Jarita faltered.

She realised that since coming to the Abbey she had not read a newspaper, although she knew that Alvaric did so.

"I see I shall have to make a list of the subjects which are essential and when I see you again I will prepare a questionnaire to make quite sure that your reading is on the right lines as it was when you were at home."

Theobold Muir looked at her disparagingly and said sharply:

"Your teachers have always spoken about you as being intelligent. You will require every ounce of brain you ever possessed to play the part I intend you to play in the future."

"Y-yes, Papa."

The words came falteringly from between Jarita's lips as if he compelled her to speak them.

"And the first thing you can do," Theobold Muir said as he looked down at Bobo, "is to get rid of that unpleasant and dangerous animal. Keep it in a cage if it amuses you and pay servants to look after it, but do not come in personal contact with it. That, Jarita, is an order!"

"Y-yes . . . Papa."

She had to agree. It was impossible to defy him.

Without waiting for her to rise, Theobold Muir turned and walked from the terrace into the Abbey.

Jarita knew she ought to follow, to see him to the front door and wave good-bye when he drove away in his carriage, but it was impossible to move.

Instead she picked up Bobo and hid her face in his fur.

"Oh, Bobo . . . Bobo . . . what am I to . . . do?" she whispered.

Then the tears came.

*     *     *

Lord Vernham, returning home towards the Abbey, pushed Black Knight into moving faster than the great stallion had ever moved before.

The consultation at North Farm had in fact taken far longer than he had intended and now he knew that Jarita would wonder what had happened to him and why he was so late.

He was anxious to see her again.

He thought that if he had realised how much there was to be done at the farm he would have delayed his visit until the following day, when they could have gone there together.

As the foreman had said, owing to damp and neglect, a vital wall of the farm had collapsed and it was not now a question of renovation but of rebuilding the whole place.

It had to be done, but it would cost a lot of money and the workmen could not have changed the plans without his approval.

As Black Knight, sweating from the speed at which he had galloped, brought Lord Vernham to the front door of the Abbey, it was half after five.

'I hope Jarita did not wait tea for me,' he thought.

He walked into the house to find the usual array of footmen in the Hall.

"Where is Her Ladyship?"

"She is in the Long Gallery, M'Lord."

Lord Vernham went up the stairs two at a time.

He only wished that Jarita was as eager to see him as he was to see her.

She filled his mind to the point where he felt like a young boy with his first love, so eager, so ardent, so infatuated that it was hard for him to think of anything else but his wife.

The Long Gallery was one of the most beautiful features of the house.

Halfway down the Gallery there was a huge stone mediaeval fireplace in front of which were two large sofas.

There were portraits of Vernes on the walls, there were flags that had been captured in the various battles in which they had fought, besides a collection of priceless china that had been specially made for the Abbey two centuries earlier.

Jarita was sitting forlornly on one of the sofas with the tea-things in front of her—the silver tea-pot and kettle, on an ornate tray the fine porcelain cups and the dishes on which was every sort of delicacy.

There was also, Lord Vernham saw at once, a large birthday-cake on which his name and age were inscribed in pink icing.

"Forgive me, Jarita," he apologised. "I did my best to hurry back as I promised, but things were far worse at the farm than I had expected."

He was walking towards her as he spoke. Then as he reached the tea-table and looked down at her sitting behind it his expression changed and he asked quickly:

"What has happened? What has upset you?"

He thought for one moment that Bobo must have died or been run over. He could not imagine anything else that would make her look as she did.

"It is . . . nothing," she answered dully. "I am very glad you are . . . back."

Lord Vernham sat down on the sofa beside her and took her hand in his.

"Something has disturbed you—I want to know what it is."

She shook her head but her lips trembled and she turned her eyes away from him.

"You have to tell me, Jarita," he said. "When I left you were so happy. Can it be that you are angry with me for not coming back as soon as I hoped to do?"

"N-no . . . no . . . it is not that."

"Then what is it?"

He thought she would not be able to answer him, but as if the words were dragged from her she said after a moment:

"P-Papa . . . called to . . . see me."

Lord Vernham stiffened.

This was something he had not expected.

"Your father? What has he said to upset you like this?"

"I cannot . . . tell you."

"You must tell me," he insisted.

Then even as he spoke he saw the fear in her eyes and knew that was the wrong approach.

An instinct such as he never disobeyed warned him she was terrified and as he looked at her he realized that she was wild and panic-striken as she had been when he first married her.

But of what?

Surely she realised that her father had no jurisdiction over her now that she was married, and physically it was impossible for him to hurt her.

Nevertheless, it was obvious that for the moment Jarita had no wish to confide in him.

With an effort, because he knew it was the right approach, Lord Vernham made himself say:

"A cake! Have you really ordered a birthday-cake for me, Jarita? I do not believe I have had one since I was at Eton."

"I . . . I hope you . . . like it."

"It was wonderful of you to think of it," he said, "and I am sure the Chef would be very disappointed if we do not cut it."

He rose from the sofa as he spoke and cut the cake, putting one slice on a plate for Jarita and one for himself.

As he sat down again he felt something rubbing against his leg and saw it was Bobo.

He bent to pat the cub and said:

"I think really I am cross with Bobo for not looking after you when I was away. If he had done his job properly you would not have such a woebegone expression and I should have been welcomed in the way I have grown to look forward to and expect."

"I am . . . sorry," Jarita murmured.

He thought she was near to tears but she busied herself pouring out his tea.

"It is not too strong?" she asked anxiously.

"I am prepared to take it as it comes," he answered. "I realize it must have been standing for some time."

"I th-thought you would be back by . . . half past four."

"Your father did not stay to tea?"

"No."

"Why did he call?"

"He has been in . . . London until now."

"Did he leave any message for me?"

"No."

She was making things very difficult, Lord Vernham thought, but he knew it was not intentional. Something had happened to turn her from the smiling, happy woman he had left after luncheon to the frightened creature she was now.

He looked at her without making it obvious he was doing so and knew there was the expression on her face which he had seen before and which he had hoped never to see again.

He ate a few mouthfuls of the cake and set it down on the plate.

"That was delicious!" he said. "Have you any more surprises for me this evening?"

"I . . . I am . . . afraid not."

"Then perhaps you would like to hear a little of my book either before or after dinner? All the way home I was thinking of how much you would enjoy the story of the two elephants who loved each other so devotedly."

Jarita got to her feet.

"No!" she cried. "No, I cannot hear . . . about them today . . . not today!"

Her hand went up to her eyes and she turned and ran from the Long Gallery before Lord Vernham could stop her.

Only when he was alone did he feel an urge for the first time in his life to murder a man, and he thought perhaps it was a good thing that Theobold Muir was not present.

\*     \*     \*

Jarita tossed and turned in her bed and found it impossible to sleep.

She told herself despairingly that she had ruined her husband's birthday-dinner.

She had spoilt what she had looked forward to so excitedly, their time together, simply because she could not escape from the misery and horror that her father had brought with him.

It was easy to tell herself with her brain that what her father suggested would not take place for a year or perhaps longer.

But the thought of Alvaric leaving her, going away as her father had said he would, back to the women he loved and who loved him, was an unspeakable agony.

"How can I bear it? How can I let him go?" Jarita asked herself, and wanted to cry out at the pain that such an idea evoked.

"I want him to stay with me . . . and I want him . . ."

She stopped suddenly.

The thought which had come to her mind made her sit up in bed.

Almost like a blinding light, almost as if what she was thinking was written in words of fire in the darkness, of the wall opposite her, she knew what she wanted.

She wanted her husband to love her!

Not until this moment—and now she knew she had been very stupid—had it entered her head that it was not friendship she was asking of him—but love.

"I love . . . him!" she said wonderingly, and could not imagine how she had been so obtuse, so stupid, as not to realise it sooner.

"I love him! I love him!"

She said the words aloud and they were so sensational that she could not believe they were really on her lips.

Now as if a light came to disperse the darkness with which she had been encompassed everything was very clear.

She had loved Lord Vernham, she thought, even though she had felt afraid of him, when he had been so understanding and kind after she had tried to drown herself. And every day she had grown to love him more and more.

She trusted him, because he gave her sympathy and understanding and a sense of safety and security such as she had never known.

But all the time what she had been feeling and what had been growing within her until it filled her whole being was love!

She had not realised that love was like this—a happiness which could yet be an agony because she was afraid of losing him.

Now the thought came to her that while she loved him he would never love her.

What had she to offer him? What could she mean to him except a woman who like a tiresome, untamed animal would not always do what he wanted?

Because everything that she was feeling was so revolutionary Jarita lit the candles by her bed, then walked across the room to light the one on the dressing-table.

She wanted to look at her face to see first if she looked any different because she was in love, and secondly to ask herself desperately if she had anything which could attract the man she had married.

'If only I were beautiful,' she thought, and saw her eyes staring back at her with a look of despair in them.

She walked about the bed-room restlessly, and Bobo, who had been sleeping on the end of her bed, woke up to stare at her, wondering why she was not quiet as she usually was.

For once Jarita hardly noticed him.

She felt as if her whole body was pulsating in a manner which had made it come alive and made her feel quite different from the person she had been before.

"I am in love," she told herself wonderingly, "in love, and I want him! I want to be with him . . . I want him to . . . kiss me."

For a moment she was almost shocked at her own thoughts, then she remembered how he had kissed her hand and she wondered if it had ever crossed his mind that he might kiss her lips.

"Oh, Alvaric, I love you!"

She felt as if her thoughts winged towards him in the next room and even as she did so there came a knock on the door.

It was the outer door which led to the lobby and

after a moment's hesitation she crossed the room to open it.

It was Holden who stood there.

"What is it, Holden?" she asked.

"I'm sorry to disturb you, Your Ladyship," Holden replied. "I was going to His Lordship's room, but as his light's out I know he's asleep."

"Do not disturb him," Jarita said. "His Lordship had a long day and I am sure he is tired."

"That's what I thought, Your Ladyship, but I thinks perhaps I should tell you what's happened, just in case later you speak to His Lordship."

"Something is wrong?"

"It's only a warning like," Holden replied, "but we've just been informed by someone from the village that a lion's escaped from a circus which was travelling towards St. Albans."

"And you think it might come here?" Jarita asked.

"There's always the chance, seeing as there's other lions about," Holden answered, "but I hopes, M'Lady, I hopes very much he won't!"

"Why?"

"Because they say he's dangerous. Struck down his keeper, he did, and badly mauled two other people as got in his way when he was escaping."

Holden paused to say impressively:

"They talk of him as being a killer, and anyone who sees him should shoot on sight!"

"That sounds frightening!" Jarita exclaimed.

"That's why I think His Lordship ought to know," Holden said, "but I won't disturb him. If he wakes, M'Lady, give him this."

As Holden spoke he held out a long-barrelled rifle.

He gave it into her hands, saying as he did so:

"It's what His Lordship used in Africa. But be careful, Your Ladyship. It's loaded."

"Yes, of course, and I will tell His Lordship what you said."

"Thank you, Your Ladyship. Sorry to have disturbed you."

"That is quite all right, Holden."

Jarita closed the door, then propped the rifle against the table beside her bed.

Holden had been right not to wake his master.

She had thought when she left him after dinner that it had been a drawn-out meal with long silences because she had found it impossible to talk naturally, although Lord Vernham had tried to interest her in a number of subjects.

"I am going to bed," she said miserably as they moved into the Salon.

She longed to stay with him, and yet at the same time she was afraid of breaking down, afraid that because she was so unhappy she would be weak enough to tell him everything her father had said.

She could imagine nothing that could be more embarrassing or perhaps more conducive to making Lord Vernham decided to go away even sooner than her father predicted.

She told herself that whatever happened she must keep silent, and yet it had been hard and almost impossible to sit beside him and not tell him how apprehensive she was of the future.

She had in fact only been in her own room for about an hour when she heard him come up to his own.

She listened to him moving about until finally he got into bed and his light had gone out.

It was then that she too had tried to sleep only to find it impossible.

Now she blew out the candles and looked to see if there was a light under the communicating door.

"If he wakes," she told herself, "it will be an excuse to go into his room."

She remembered how kind he had been when she and Bobo were frightened by the thunder-storm.

She wondered what he would say if she got into his bed and asked him to hold her in his arms.

She felt a little thrill run through her at the thought. Then her heart dropped at the idea that he would do so only because he was kind and not because he wanted to.

"I want him to love me! I want him to love me!" Jarita said over and over again, with her eyes on the door which separated them.

\*　\*　\*

Lord Vernham awoke with the alertness of a man who was used to sensing danger.

As he did so he realised that what had aroused him was the roaring of the lions in their enclosure.

It was unusual, for actually since they had been in their new home they had been very quiet.

Now they were making the most unaccountable noise and he thought, although he was not sure, that it sounded as if they had been disturbed and were not only roaring but snarling.

Lord Vernham wondered what could have upset them.

He could not believe there were strangers walking about in the Park at night, but if there were they would certainly disturb Bella and she would be ready to protect her cubs.

It would definitely be wise to find out what was happening.

He jumped out of bed, lit one of the candles, found a shirt in the drawer and a pair of trousers in the wardrobe, and hastily put them on.

Knowing the ground was dry, he slipped his feet into the velvet slippers which Jarita had given him as a birthday-present, before he quietly opened the door of his room and hurried downstairs.

It was easier to leave the house in the direction he

wished to go by opening one of the windows that led onto the terrace.

As he stepped outside he could hear the lions sounding even more ferocious, and he moved quickly across the lawns down towards the bridge which spanned the lake at the end of the garden.

It was easy to see his way, for the moon was full, casting a mystical silvery light on the still lake.

At any other time Lord Vernham would have wanted to stand and admire the beauty of it. But now he was worried, for the nearer he got to the lions the more he realised that something very unusual was occurring.

Bella was certainly snarling and he knew that she was not only angry but also on the defensive.

If there was anybody in the enclosure she would charge them and undoubtedly kill them.

Lord Vernham hurried across the bridge which led into the Park and now that he was close to the enclosure the noise was almost deafening.

Ajax was roaring too, and as if they had been aroused by the lions, the cheetahs were joining in.

He went towards the gate which led into the enclosure and knew from the violence with which Bella was snarling that he must establish his identity before he entered; otherwise they would be liable to pounce on him.

"Bella!" he called. "Ajax! What has upset you?"

At the sound of his voice Ajax stopped roaring, although Bella still went on growling but on a lower note.

"Come here! Come to me," Lord Vernham said. "Come and tell me what is the matter. Come on, Bella. Nothing shall hurt you. What has made you angry?"

He saw as he spoke that Ajax was coming towards him, but Bella was standing in front of the wooden house where he thought her cubs must be, snarling ferociously and on the defensive.

"What is it?" he asked.

He put his hand on the gate as he spoke, ready to open it, and as he did so he heard a movement in the thick clump of bushes to the right of him.

"Who is there? What are you doing?'

The question was sharp.

Again there was a movement, but it was hard to see, because the bushes were in the shadow, whether it was a man or a boy who was causing so much trouble.

"Come out and let me see you," Lord Vernham ordered.

Ajax had reached the gate by now. He was emitting a low growling sound which vibrated in his throat.

Once again there was a movement in the shrubs, then suddenly into the moonlight so that Lord Vernham could see it clearly came a large lion.

It was old and mangy but obviously dangerous, and it stood looking at him for a moment, then began to advance stealthily. Lord Vernham knew it was stalking him, ready for the final spring.

He stood absolutely still, his body tense but completely controlled, watching the lion, well aware that to speak would not help and might even galvanise the animal into quicker action.

Too late he realised that to have come here as he had without a weapon of any sort in his hand had been rash and unprofessional; but he had never for a moment thought that in his own quiet Park-land there could be danger outside the enclosure.

Ajax was growling angrily and the lion approaching Lord Vernham came a little nearer, then seemed to tense its lean body, every muscle braced for the kill.

Lord Vernham drew in his breath, wondering how quickly he could move aside, knowing that it would be a question of avoiding the lion's outstretched claws in the split second that he was in the air.

Then as he thought there would in fact be no escape and he would be mauled even if he was not killed, there was a loud explosion.

It came from behind him, a report; because it was so unexpected, it seemed almost world-shattering, and even as the lion sprang, it collapsed on the ground.

For a moment Lord Vernham could only stare at the twitching body, knowing that never in his life had he been nearer to death and finding it hard to realise that the danger was over and he was unharmed.

Then a rifle was thrown down at his feet and Jarita's arms were round his neck. She was kissing his face wildly and frantically with tight, frightened lips.

"I thought he would . . . kill you!" she was saying over and over again. "I thought he would . . . kill you!"

Wonderingly, feeling as if he were in a dream, the explosion from the shot still ringing in his ears, Lord Vernham put his arms round her.

Then his mouth came down on hers and held her captive.

# Chapter Seven

Lord Vernham's arms tightened crushingly round Jarita until she could hardly breathe, yet his lips brought her everything she had longed for and swept away even her terror that he might have been killed.

He raised his head, looked down at her face in the moonlight, and said:

"You saved my life, my darling!"

She drew his head a little closer to hers. Her body was soft and trembling and he realised she was wearing only a nightgown and that her feet were bare.

He glanced towards the motionless body of the lion.

"I will take you home," he said gently, and lifted her up in his arms.

She did not answer, she only looked up at him and he thought that her eyes held the light of the stars in them as he carried her across the bridge and onto the other side of the lake.

Here where the garden had not yet been cleared the grass had grown high. It was filled with flowers and the fragrance of them seemed to mingle with the moonlight reflected on the lake and the beauty of the Abbey standing above them.

Lord Vernham hesitated for a moment, then he laid

Jarita gently on the grass and threw himself down beside her.

"You saved my life!" he said again. "How did you know? How were you aware of what was happening?"

"It was my . . . fault that you went . . . out without knowing there was . . . an escaped lion in the neighbourhood," she replied. "Holden told me . . . but I . . . went to sleep."

There was so much self-accusation in her voice that Lord Vernham bent forward to put his cheek against hers.

"You came after me and saved me. It was very brave of you."

"If you had . . . died . . . I would have . . . died too."

The words were hardly above a whisper, but he heard them.

"Forget it," he said. "We are both alive, and now I think perhaps you love me a little."

His lips were very close to hers and he could see the question she wanted to ask him in her eyes.

"I love you, my precious," he said. "I have loved you for a long time but I was afraid to tell you so."

"You . . . love me? You really . . . love me?"

"I love you more than I thought it possible to love any woman, but I have been so afraid—desperately afraid of frightening you."

"I am . . . not frightened of you . . . now," Jarita said, "but are you sure . . . that you . . . love me? I am not . . . dreaming?"

"I love you so overwhelmingly that I can think of nothing but you."

He felt the thrill which his words gave her flicker through her body and his hand caressed her, feeling the long line of her hips beneath the thin nightgown.

"How . . . long have you . . . loved me . . ?"

His touch gave her such strange sensations that the breath came fitfully between her lips.

"I fell in love with you when I brought you out of the well."

"Why did . . . you not . . . tell . . . me?"

"You trusted me as a friend, but what I felt for you, my lovely one, was not friendship. It has driven me crazy not to be able to kiss you and to make you mine."

Lord Vernham's voice seemed to vibrate on the last word.

"You wanted to kiss me?"

"More than I ever wanted anything in my whole life."

"But you . . . did not . . . try . . ."

"I was so afraid of frightening you."

There was a little silence, then Jarita whispered:

"You said . . . you wanted . . . to make me . . . yours."

He could hardly hear the words.

"God knows that is what I want, but I could not bear to frighten you!"

"You will not do . . . that . . . and I want . . . to be . . .yours."

"My perfect darling. I will be very gentle."

His lips sought hers.

His kiss was at first slow, light, and tender, almost as if he wooed her.

Then when he felt her respond, when something magical rose in them both, his mouth became more demanding, insistent, passionate.

Jarita felt as if a flickering flame was burning through her body and the wonder of it was part of the moonlight, the stars reflected in the lake, the fragrance of the grasses and the beauty of the Abbey.

They were one with Lord Vernham, his arms, his hands, his lips!

Her whole body vibrated to the sensations he aroused in her and to the rapture that joined them until they were no longer two people, but one.

The stars fell down to cover them, the rustle in the grass joined the music in their hearts, and their souls touched the divine.

Then in the silence there was a soft, sweet cry, but it was not one of fear.

* * *

Later, very much later, when outside the Abbey the stars were fading in the sky, Jarita lifted her face from her husband's shoulder to whisper:

"Do you . . . still love me?"

"Do you really need to ask such a foolish question, my adorable wife?" he replied.

He turned his head on the pillow to kiss her forehead, then he pushed aside her long fair hair so that he could touch the softness of her breast.

"I did not frighten you?" he asked.

"You know that . . . everything was . . . unbelievably wonderful . . . I did not think that . . . love could be . . . so perfect, so good and yet so . . . exciting."

"I want to excite you."

"You made me feel . . . as if I touched . . . the stars . . . and yet I was . . . wild . . . like the wind."

"That is what I want to make you feel, my precious little love."

She quivered because he was caressing her, then she whispered:

"I want to . . . ask you . . . something."

"What is it, my darling?"

"Do you . . . think that . . . you have . . . given me a baby?"

He smiled in the darkness before he replied:

"It is a possibility, but we will make quite certain if that is what you want."

She moved a little nearer to him before she said in a voice he could hardly hear:

"Papa . . . said that when I give you an . . . heir

you will leave me and go . . . abroad . . . back to the
. . . beautiful women you have . . . loved before.

She felt Lord Vernham stiffen before he said quietly:

"If I go abroad, which is very unlikely because there
is so much to do here, you will come with me."

Jarita gave a little cry.

"Do you mean that?"

"Do you think I would leave behind the most valuable and most perfect treasure I possess?"

He heard her sigh of relief before he went on:

"As for other women, my enchanting love, it is impossible for me to see anything but your large expressive eyes, your soft lips, and your exquisite, perfect
body, which excites me as I have never been excited
before!"

"I . . . need not be . . . afraid of . . . losing you?"

"I shall spend my whole life teaching you not to be
afraid and I will make sure I will never lose you. You
must know already that it is impossible for either of us
to live without the other!"

Again Jarita sighed, but this time it was a sound of
sheer happiness.

"I was . . . afraid," she said after a moment, "that
what Papa said would come . . . true."

"What else did he say?"

"When you went away, he wanted me to be . . .
hostess at Vernham House and . . . preside over a
Salon of important and distinguished people."

He felt her whole body tremble as she said:

"I should hate it! You know I would hate it! I
would be nervous and f-frightened, and Papa would
. . . dominate me as he has . . . done all my life."

"As he will never do again," Lord Vernham said
quietly. "Forget your father, Jarita. I will speak to him
and make sure that these absurd ideas of his do not
disrupt or spoil our married life."

"Do you think he will . . . listen to you?"

"He will," Lord Vernham said grimly. "You belong

to me now, Jarita. You are mine and I will take care of you in the future, so that no-one will trouble you or hurt you again. That is a promise!"

"I am . . . sorry that I spoilt your birthday," she murmured. "I had looked forward to it so much. Then when Papa said you would . . . leave me . . . I thought that you had never cared for me but only tried to be kind."

"And now you know that what I feel is very different?" he asked.

She turned to kiss his shoulder with a passionate little gesture before she answered:

"I know now I have come alive . . . that you have given me all the beauty and . . . wonder of the world. The sky, the sun, the stars, the moon, and the animals —they are all part of you."

"My darling, that is what I want you to feel," he said. "That is what we will always feel about each other, and no-one shall interfere or spoil our happiness."

Jarita knew he was speaking of her father and for the first time in her life he ceased to have any importance.

Close against her husband's heart with his arms round her she felt as if she were in a fortress which could withstand any assault.

As if he knew what she was thinking, Lord Vernham put his fingers under her chin and turned her face up towards his.

"Tell me!" he commanded.

"I . . . I was thinking that I am . . . safe with you and that I do . . . believe when you tell me . . . no-one will hurt me again as Papa . . . hurt me in the past."

"You are mine," Lord Vernham said, "and there are so many wonderful things we will do together, my dearest heart. We will increase our collection of animals, for one thing, until we have one of the best menageries in the whole of England, and we will make those we keep captive so happy that I shall write not only one book of love-stories about them, but a dozen!"

"That is a marvellous idea! I want to begin now!" Jarita cried.

"At the moment I will not allow you to think of anything but me," Lord Vernham replied, "and, my darling, we will have our own family to consider as well. The house is big enough for quite a number of our children."

"You will not . . . leave me when you have an . . . heir?"

The question was no longer so serious as when she had first asked it, and yet the fear was still there, lingering in the back of her mind.

"There is only one reason why I should ever go away."

"What is . . . that?"

He felt her body tense beneath his hands as he answered:

"If you should cease to love me."

"I shall never do that . . . you know I could never stop loving you . . . I love you with all of me . . . with my mind, my heart, and my soul."

His lips touched hers as he said:

You have forgotten something."

"What have I forgotten?"

"Your body—your beautiful, exciting body, my darling. I want that, too."

"It is yours! You know it is . . . yours!"

"My sweet—my wild, unwilling little wife, how can I tell you how much you mean to me?"

"Not unwilling. Never . . . never again will I ever be . . . unwilling to do . . . anything you want or ask of me."

His mouth came down on hers, stifling the last words, kissing her until it was impossible to think of anything but him.

Once again she felt the flame rising within her, leaping unrestrained and wilder than it had been before.

She wanted him closer and still closer to her and she knew that the ecstasy and rapture which made her feel that he swept her towards the stars was what he was feeling too.

Then his heart was beating on hers, and his lips were demanding that she surrender herself completely and absolutely to his need of her.

"I love you!" she wanted to say, and knew that the fire that consumed them both was the true eternal love which would never die.

\* \* \*

Beneath the bed a blissfully happy Bobo, having torn into pieces an expensive nightgown, a pair of trousers, and a shirt, was stalking a new prey.

He pounced on it and held it down with both his front paws in case it should escape.

A black velvet shoe embroidered with a coronet in gold thread was the best kill he had ever made.